A Touch of Reality

Best Nwachinemere

ISBN: 978-978-57058-3-6

ISBN: 978-978-57058-4-3

Published in Nigeria in 2019 by The Zuma Publishing

Yawahab Phase 3, Wuye, Abuja, Nigeria

07052088876

Contact@zumapublishing.com

www.zumapublishing.com

Cover: Weird Zesty

A catalogue of this book is available from Nigeria from the National Library of Nigeria.

To Dad, for his indescribable love.
To UC, for teaching me how to love
selflessly.
To Brian, who even now, overwhelms
me with his love.

ONE

KELECHI SHIFTED HER weight to relieve her right foot. She had been standing for seven precious minutes waiting for her Uber ride. When he arrived, he'd give a lengthy explanation of how the bad road connecting to the avenue made him late, apologizing the whole trip. A lame excuse, she'd say. The avenue wasn't the only entrance to the estate. Then she'd deduct from his payment, his cries and complaints forming nasty music to her ears as she maee her way to her office. Lucy, her secretary, would come and complete his payment. She loved playing the nice lady and would placate the driver by sympathizing with him. She believed Kelechi didn't know, but Kelechi knew, just as she knew everything going on in the office, including what they said about her behind her back. That made her efficient and productive. Lucy's type always served her type; it was how the world worked.

Today, however, was not that day. Kelechi had an important meeting that could launch her media company to the next level, which would totally sideline their rivals. She couldn't wait much longer even if she wanted to.

She adjusted her gold wristwatch, part of the jewelry set Anika, her director and mentor, had gifted her on her twenty-fifth birthday. It'd also been the day Anika had handed over the directorship to Kelechi, saying, 'I've never worked with anyone like you all through my thirty-eight years in the industry. You'll go far.'

Kelechi accepted the gift with a smile. Her hardness and tenacity were unmatched which gave her an edge. Having known the old lady would retire soon, Kelechi worked extra hard to qualify for her position. Nonetheless, she'd been beside herself with excitement when Anika made it official. That was four years ago, and ever since, Kelechi always wore at least one piece of the jewelry, not just because she loved them, but because the watch, necklace, bracelets, and earrings represented the transition from her old position to her new title.

'Maybe I should have accepted my neighbor's offer to drive me.' She recalled the exchange from a few minutes ago.

"Hey beautiful," a man in his early thirty's said.

The idiot disturbed her a lot, unfortunately, not enough for her to report him as a stalker. She considered ignoring him, but she had done so the night before, so she humored him. "Hi."

"I called you last night." When she didn't respond, he continued, shining a new light to the term 'idiot'.

"Ah." She left it at that. No matter how stupid he seemed, at least he'd get the hint. She had heard him the night before but didn't answer just to discourage him.

Apparently, she'd hoped for a lot because the idiot continued, "Need a ride?"

She did, but not from him. "No, thanks."

"I don't mind dropping you off."

Kelechi turned and fixed her gaze on his, a trick that worked miracles when accompanied by the tone she used when she wanted something done immediately. "I said no, thank you."

No need to snap or shout. The ice in her tone made his jaw drop as he probably searched for what to say or unsay. Thankfully, he did neither and turned to his Ford. "Smart choice," she said, too low for him to hear, not that she cared if he did. The most he could do was stop talking to her or speak to her only when he absolutely had to, like her two other neighbors. Exactly as she liked it. Friendship was a huge burden.

She waved at the approaching yellow taxi. She'd waited on the sidewalk long enough. The taxi slowed, skidding to a stop about eight feet ahead.

Why couldn't he roll back and save me the stress of walking on my four-inch Jimmy Choo sandals? These shoes cost me a fortune, much more than he'd likely makes in years.

Time, however, was of the essence, and she couldn't afford to miss the ride. She did a mental evaluation. Two months of her automobile savings would score her dream ride. Then all this nonsense would end. That consolation kept her sane. Not that she couldn't afford a car, but she organized her life, down to how she saved and what she saved for. Kelechi had everything sorted out—insurance, pension savings, trust fund, and education savings (for the children she may have if she married), house, emergency, and automobile.

"Madam, where you dey go?" the cab driver asked before she opened the door.

She ignored him until she was as comfortable as she could manage in the back seat, then gave him the address. "Please roll up the window. I don't like dust." He smirked but did as she said.

"Madam, you dey work for Aso Rock?" he asked, having realized where they were going.

She snorted. "No."

He watched her from the rear-mirror, a frown creasing his features. He was too young, maybe twenty-two, and good looking to be as ignorant as he was, then shrugged, "So, wetin you dey go there go do na?"

She pressed her temples with two fingers. She didn't have to answer him, but she did anyway. "I have an appointment."

He nodded. "Na with Mr. President?"

"No."

"Ah..."

Kelechi felt heat rise to her face that the driver would dismiss the issue like that. The awe that'd dwelt on his face earlier through the rearview mirror was gone, snuffed out like candlelight. "I am going to meet the Senate president," she said, focusing on him in the mirror to gauge his reaction.

"Okay. But if you see Mr. President, please tell him to reduce the fuel price, e dey very expansive."

She rolled her eyes and sighed. "It's 'expensive'."

She watched his shoulder rise. "I no care. You know wetin I dey talk."

The man did not know the weight in the senate's position, and Kelechi couldn't blame him for that. His type likely didn't keep up with matters of the country. "Just drive and don't try too hard to understand what is above you."

Kelechi pulled out and powered her Tab to crosscheck interview questions. The driver was silent, perhaps offended. Kelechi couldn't care less.

Kelechi was excited about how well work progressed. In four short years, she'd expanded the company to include a fiction column. It'd started as a branch publishing short stories for their magazine, but recently she'd begun publishing them as books.

The thought spurred her to open the next file, a story titled 'Mistletoe', from a local girl. She leaned back expecting a love story. If the story was as good as the girl's blurb, she'd found a gem. She couldn't have been more right. Three sentences in, she forced herself to come up for breath. It was so deep and as real as the tears forming in her eyes.

She looked out the window to get herself together because she was supposed to read critically. But her gaze met an unfamiliar landscape. She snapped her face forward and met the driver's gaze through the rear-view. Her heart leaped out of its confines, slapping against her chest as blood roared in her ears. His face was as hard as a soldier's, his jaw protruding to a peak and his lips so tight deep lines fanned his mouth.

"Where are you going?" So immersed in her work was she that she'd lost track of time. Kelechi calibrated her geography of Abuja, trying to remember which part was agrestic. The road was barely wide enough for the taxi, causing branches of low-hanging guavas to brush the windows on both sides. How she'd missed the rustic scenery was a mystery, and worse, it blinded her from spotting any landmarks.

Panic set in. When she rode in buses, Kelechi was cautious, but many years of taking taxis that carried only her made her comfortable enough to never take the kidnapping stories she reported to heart. They were just headlines.

She grappled for the door and window, but neither budged. She stole a glance in the mirror. The driver smirked at her.

"Please, where are you taking me?" Kelechi's voice was shaky. When he didn't answer, she lunged at him, hoping to wrestle the steering wheel from him, but with one arm he smacked her down.

She tasted copper. For over a decade, no one, not even her parents or teachers, had laid a hand on her. The rage overpowered her fear, pouring from her hands to his neck as she cinched the chain handle of her newest Manolo bag around his throat and pulled with a strength she hadn't used in a long time.

He let go of the wheel and tried to pry the chain from his throat, but she wouldn't let go. The car swerved from one side of the road to the other, crushing grasses as it went farther into the shoulder of the road. Her palms sweat and her wrist ached, yet she held fast. A hot white light blinded her, her head feeling like it'd split before warm liquid flowed down. The driver had struck her with an iron. She released the chain and tried to focus her vision, but all she saw was a sea of inky blackness.

TWO

KELECHI'S HEAD HURT, her back ached, and her waist screamed of discomfort. She lay in an awkward angle on the floor of the vehicle. Little wonder why her every joint was in excruciating pain. Kelechi couldn't summon up the energy required to rearrange her body. It was by sheer will she snaked out her arm to feel for her tablet. She needed to send out an SOS and enable her device location. She was infuriated with herself for not thinking of that earlier.

Kelechi liked to think she acted indifferent during crisis situations, but apparently, she'd never faced a dire situation before.

The beat of 'One Love', her ringtone was encouragement enough for her to move. But the driver had her phone and her bag on the passenger seat.

Kelechi racked her brain thinking of the next step. *I should have accepted Mr. Neighbor's ride. Or waited for the Uber.* Actually, this whole thing wouldn't have happened if she'd tapped a little from her main savings and completed her automobile savings.

How long before someone noticed her absence? On a normal day, it'd be noticed immediately, but because of her appointment at Aso Rock, Lucy had left her schedule open, as they weren't sure how long the interview would take. Therefore, no one would notice if she didn't show up to work at all.

Lucy had been the one to set up the appointment. Occasionally, she did things that Kelechi totally approved of, but Kelechi decided yesterday that Lucy couldn't handle the interview.

Who apologized when someone bumps into them and as a result got liquid spilled on their clumsy selves? Lucy had done exactly that when the journalist had bumped into her yesterday. She had no backbone, and that was a fault. Kelechi couldn't trust her to handle the pigheaded Secretary of State.

"But this is my gig!" Lucy had protested.

"What makes it your gig?"

"I know what I went through to get the appointment."

If it'd been a test, Lucy had failed. Mentioning she went through whatever to land a gig was unprofessional, and in their line of business, whatever connection you used to get what you wanted was fair. It was your duty to get them. "Who is the director here?"

Kelechi had smiled when the older woman bowed her head. She was right. Lucy was just too soft. "You, ma."

Kelechi had thought she detected an unusual force in the 'ma', but she let it go. She wouldn't though if it happened again. It was one thing to gossip about her behind her back, but it was another to disrespect her to her face. "Good, now you are excused."

"You got a personal call earlier, ma."

When she asked to be excused, she liked them to be obeyed instantly. Maybe Lucy was trying to act up. She opened her mouth to lecture her, but Lucy was already talking.

"It was from your brother. He said your mother isn't feeling too well."

"Call him and tell him I'm busy with work, but I'll call them when I get a chance."

"OK, ma'am. May I come with you, ma?"

"Lucy, leave my office."

Maybe she should have accepted to take Lucy with her. That way if she didn't make it, Lucy would raise alarm.

You know if you had just let her go for the interview alone, you wouldn't be in this situation now, the annoying little voice said. She had mastered ignoring the voice, so she did. But it had more to say. *Or if you had accepted the neighbor's kind offer*. She didn't think back because doing so felt like having a conversation with the voice, which was useless since the voice was intent on tearing apart her perspective.

After a while, when she thought the voice was back to wherever hole it crawled out from, it said again, *did you later call to find out about your mother?* She'd meant to, and after she was out, she would even go visit her. But she didn't care for the voice's judgmental tone, as if not calling yesterday made her a bad child. Instead, she focused on the issue at hand. Each moment brought her farther from town.

She wondered how much the driver would demand. He probably wasn't a professional kidnapper and had abducted her because of her connection to Aso Rock. Kelechi was sad that she had to part with her hard-earned money for the fool, but anything was worth her freedom.

"How much do you want?" she asked. When it became apparent, he wouldn't answer, she added, "One hundred thousand Naira?" At his scoff he doubled it, "Two hundred thousand?" Silence. "One million?" Silence. She wanted to raise the bar but thought otherwise. He might mute because that's what he expected her to do. Kelechi wouldn't play into his hands. She was too smart for that. If he wanted silence, she'd give it to him, and they both knew who ran the show.

After minutes that seemed more like hours, she broke. Dense forest surrounded them, and they weren't traveling on a road anymore. They were amid wilderness, going God knew where. "Oga, two million na." She expected action at this, but not the one she got. The driver turned up the car radio volume, leaving her to worry herself to an early grave.

She checked her wristwatch for the time. 11:22. She must've gone down hard to be unaware so much time and passed. Her meeting was over. Rage blinded her. She had a very important job she did for the country and the world, and she worked hard at her job, and some ignorant cab driver was ruining it, for what, money? She didn't realize she'd balled her hands into fists until the artificial nail on her middle finger bent, hurting her. At that point, she'd die if it meant killing him too.

Kelechi eyed the iron he'd slammed into her skull and calculated how to nab it. Just before she lunged, he slowed the car and stopped.

"Why are we stopping?" Another kind of fear had crushed her soul, one she never fathomed she'd face. She backed into the corner of the car and clamped her legs shut. Kidnapping her was bad enough; raping her was a whole new shade of worse.

He got off the vehicle, and Kelechi seized the opportunity and ran out after him, calculating the chances of escaping before he got the chance to do whatever he was planning. She'd die before letting him have his way with her. He unbuckled his belt. Kelechi's palms were clammy, and she felt cold, in contrast with the sunny weather.

He'd parked the car in the middle of the tiny clearing that served as a road. Not that there was another option considering the road was so narrow that part of the tire squashed the grass at the shoulder.

Her feet developed a mind of their own as they crisscrossed each other going backward. Oddly, the driver didn't notice. It was almost like he didn't care what she did or didn't do. Instead, he unzipped, fished out his penis, and aimed, and she realized that he was pressed.

Trying not to make any sudden movements until she was out of arm's reach, and balancing it with making enough progress so that before his zipper finally got to the end, she would have gotten far enough to make a run for it, Kelechi said all the prayers she remembered.

Then she bumped into a soft wall that developed hands and held her down. "Welcome," the wall which turned out to be a man, said.

The hands holding her were albinoid. For a moment, Kelechi thought he was talking to her, until her driver answered, turning to face them, "Thanks. Can I have my money now?"

"You will collect it when you come again."

"That was not the agreement. You told me that last time and the one before that too. It is now seven trips, and I demand my fourteen million, after which, I'm out." The illiterate kidnapper who didn't know the difference between 'expansive' and 'expensive' spoke good English. Kelechi would've bet her last kobo the day couldn't get more surprising.

"I suspected you'd say that." The albino released her as he spoke. "I have your money, have had it all along, and would have given it to you. Only you keep saying the wrong things, and now you mentioned quitting. Before you were recruited, I'm sure they told you 'out' isn't a language we speak." His voice was level and emotionless like he was talking to himself.

Kelechi couldn't see the albino because she had her back to him, but the look on her kidnapper's face was enough to tell her that if he were the devil, the man standing behind her was something bigger than the devil. Even as his knees bent and tears spilled from his eyes, she knew what was about to happen without having to hear the deafening bang that made birds take flight and her eardrums ring to the tune of a million bees. As she watched the thumb-sized hole in his chest and the red rivulet flowing from it, she didn't know who to pray to or what to pray for. Kelechi's legs weakened, and she felt the ground drop from under her.

❋❋❋

The warmth had given way to a chill which affected her insides more than her flesh. Her shirt stuck to her skin, slick with sweat. Once again, she was in the back of a car, and by the wideness of the seat, she could tell it wasn't the same vehicle as before. While the latter had been narrow, this was wide enough she could lie on her back. Kelechi didn't know how she got there, but she remembered everything else, especially the fear on the cab driver's face when the albino pulled the gun and the tears running down his face even as he took his last breath. Kelechi knew that people died, even people she knew had died, but no one had ever died in her presence, much less while she watched. She didn't even know his name, and she couldn't decide whether or not he deserved his fate.

The darkness in the vehicle prevented her from seeing past her new driver's bright skin, which meant he wouldn't know she was awake if she didn't move. Kelechi didn't know what he'd do, but whatever it was, she wasn't ready to face it.

His presence threw a different light on her predicament. She tried to think of work, of family, of anything. But she could think of nothing beyond seven trips, fourteen million Naira. It meant the driver got two million, or at least he was supposed to get two million for one victim. If that was his share alone, how much would the albino collect? And how much did they intend to ask for her ransom? A million questions buzzed around her head, none sticking long enough to get an answer before another took over.

After an eternity of bouncing around in the car, the honking of the vehicle alerted Kelechi that they had finally gotten to their destination. She sat up, preparing for whatever may come. She heard shouting and clamoring from afar and sent a silent prayer of thanks. She was grateful that wherever they were, at least there was civilization. Lights from over a dozen sources came on, scanning the car and the environment. Kelechi looked around, noticing the speed they traveled. Wherever they were, it was very far from Abuja. She needed something to mark the place—a feature or a tree or something—just in case. However, the surrounding jungle's tall trees and lush leaves were so dense that they made the one she saw earlier in the day a joke.

The gigantic red gate opened, admitting them into another world, a world of odor.

What seemed like a compound was illuminated by two yellow bulbs, Kelechi couldn't breathe through her nose, the stench suffocating. The driver, however, seemed unaffected. He got out, opened the door, grabbed her arm and pulled her up, then shoved her out onto a heap of—what were those? She jumped when something moved under her feet, reeled and fell on another moving something. Kelechi tried to make out what she was up against, but the electric bulb cast more shadows than light. Something curled around her ankle and she screamed like her life depended on it, and maybe it did. A masculine silhouette approached, torchlight preceding him. She took advantage of the bright ray and examined her surroundings.

Bile rose in her throat. By sheer will, she held down the vomit threatening to erupt. Littered like dead fishes were bodies, some sitting, others lying, just like the skeletal something under her. She got up as fast as she could while dodging them, but they didn't seem to mind as she inevitably stepped on some, they just coiled tighter.

"Hey, you, find space sidon, I no wan hear shout again for here," the silhouette barked.

"Where is this place and what are these?" she asked, gesturing around.

"Which kind question be that na? I look like your papa wey you go dey ask rubbish?"

He turned to go, taking the light with him, but not before Kelechi fully saw what she was in the midst of. They were crazy if they thought they'd jam her with those things. "You can't possibly leave me here!"

But when the man continued without sparing her a glance, she knew she had to change strategy. "I'm scared," she whined, in the tiniest voice she could muster. "Please take me with you." All men fell for the weak woman, and he'd be no different.

He halted, then turned and walked toward her. Kelechi didn't mind where he took her because she was confident that she'd find her way out of any situation. She just would rather be anywhere else than the midst of death.

"Hey, wetin dey work you? Them give you tramadol before them bring you? See, as you see me so, I no want headache. If you know wetin go dey good for you, make you shut that your dirty mouth and sidon quiet for there. If not, hmmm."

Kelechi couldn't believe what she was hearing. It was one thing to threaten her, but another to keep her against her will. And calling her dirty was out of the question. She weighed her options—choose her battles or give him a piece of her mind and risk whatever threat he'd veiled. But the image of blood soaking the brown t-shirt of the driver and the indifference of the shooter kept her in check. This new guy may not have the clearance to terminate a two million naira plus life. Still, she couldn't risk it. She'd choose her battles.

He took another step towards her, apparently awaiting her decision. Kelechi didn't need to be told twice. She found a space a few feet from the bodies and sat. This man would pay for making her sit on the bare sand, even if it meant emptying her savings.

Kelechi slept that night even though she couldn't risk it. She didn't know what woke her—the sun on her face or the ear-splitting scream—but she woke all right and wished she hadn't.

Seeing the bodies in the dark was one thing. Seeing them in the light of day was a whole new terror. There were about two dozen of them, comprising men, women, adults, and children. None seemed interested in the happenings around them. They were all bony, their eyes sunken and lifeless.

The scream sounded again, forcing her to look away from the painful sight of humans becoming bags of bones, alive. Far to her left, six heavily armed men covered in blood and sweat chopped, washed, sorted, and bagged. You'd think they were bagging ready-to-sell flour. A foot away from the six, a seventh man positioned his machete on the neck of a girl of maybe sixteen. She bowed her head like she had been waiting for this moment. She didn't even try to fight even though she was not shackled. She neither screamed nor cried. Without hesitation, the seventh man hacked her head off the shoulder. Before Kelechi's eyes, the other men took the twitching body and set to work. That was what they were bagging. She turned away and emptied her stomach.

THREE

KELECHI FELT LIKE her intestines were struggling to escape. The gray matter pouring from her mouth splattered on the helpless humans lying about, but the owners of the bodies didn't seem to notice or mind. Not that it changed anything, because she couldn't have moved even if it meant her freedom. She bent over and held onto her knee for support as she retched.

When she was relieved enough to look up, she found a thin black man looking down at her. At five feet one inch, she got that a lot which was why she'd developed a technique to match up. Her body reacted accordingly. Kelechi squared her shoulders and stood as straight as her hurting abdomen allowed and stared at the man right in his eyes. Either he didn't notice her confident pose, or he didn't care. He just continued to look at her as if he didn't see her at all. Without realizing it, she averted her gaze and focused on the ammunition slung over his shoulder and the gun hanging from his waist. The flatness of his eyes made Kelechi uncomfortable.

"You're the new arrival?" he asked.

Hate shone in Kelechi's eyes. She wanted to clamp her fingers around his neck and squeeze until he became limp. They kidnapped her and had just wasted a life, yet here he was talking like she was there by choice. She wanted to state her annoyance at being forced to stay with the smelly dying bodies. She wanted to complain about being exposed all night without food or drink, but common sense told her she might risk making a bad situation worse.

She closed her eyes and counted to ten, a trick that never failed to calm her. When she opened them, she made sure they were as devoid of emotions as his were. "Who do I negotiate my freedom with?"

"Follow me."

As he led the way towards the lengthy building, another scream tore through the air, short and weak, but as familiar as the sound of the machete slicing through flesh and bone. Kelechi heaved a sigh expelling air she didn't know she had been holding. She couldn't walk fast enough as they made their way to the building. She couldn't even look back at the people she left behind or the activity going on at the other end of the yard, she just wanted to get out of that pit, and fast. She had been afraid that she'd end up like those people wasting there. Those victims probably couldn't afford their ransom. Thankfully, she could call her secretary and Lucy would oversee the gathering of funds or the mobilizing of her family if the demand was much. Kelechi would never be among those rotting alive or being hacked into pieces. That was why she'd put in so much time and effort in work.

The building was a seemingly endless block of a wickedly high fence that reminded Kelechi of the walls of Jericho, with doors at about five ft from one another going all the way to where she couldn't see. She spotted figures on the roof, probably sentries no doubt armed better than the devil.

The guard led her to one of the doors, which opened after the first knock. He exchanged a slight nod with the man who opened the door, then entered and took a seat. The chairs in the small room were all occupied, and the only space to sit was on a bench… between two men. Both wore black shirts that Kelechi could bet hadn't seen water or soap in months. As they puffed on the wrap wedged between their fingers and exhaled clouds of smoke, which further added to the choking odor of sweat, smoke and something else she didn't care to identify, they looked like they were in their first trimester of madness, with their eyes as bloodshot as though suffering from conjunctivitis, their lips so black like charcoal was rubbed on them. One would think that they were chosen because of the similarities in their features; rough hair, bad skin, dirty hands with broken, even dirtier nails.

Of the eight men in the tiny windowless room, only the one who'd brought her looked marginally sane. Kelechi started to suggest that he sit with his friends to free up the chair he occupied, but a door opened at the other end of the room, bringing in much needed fresh air. Only the air wasn't fresh. It smelled of rotten meat yet was better than the choking confine they had subjected her to.

After this, I will take a weeklong vacation on an island. But that will be after visiting the doctor and going to the spa.

The man who brought her said, nodding towards the man who just entered. "Follow him." Even without his suggestion, she would have.

The compound on the other side of the wall looked disturbingly like the one she'd stayed in overnight. A round and high fence surrounded it, devoid of trees or anything. Just a large clearing with a scaffold, like the one in the outer yard, at one end, and people on the other. Only this time, a different activity was happening on the platform, and Kelechi couldn't decide if it was worse than what she'd witnessed at the outer yard. A woman was bathing on the stage. She seemed not to mind the guards standing at strategic points or the men and women sitting under a canopy at the other end of the yard just. Kelechi had only ever heard of this kind of shamelessness. She wished for a camera because this spectacle would dominate the headlines for days.

The guard turned back towards another door in the row. Like on the other side, the doors ran the width of the fence-building. "Where are you going?" Kelechi asked. He paused, the only indication that he'd heard her, and she continued, "Wait, you can't leave me here, haba."

"There," he said, pointing at the chattering group of people.

"No, I can't wait another minute. Take me to your leader. I want to negotiate my ransom."

"Your ransom?" he bared pure white teeth. "How did that get into your head?"

"Excuse you. I want to talk to whoever is in charge."

"Go over there, you'll be attended to when your time comes."

With that, he left, ignoring all her protests. The sun was already overhead, and it surprised Kelechi she still stood. Her stomach rumbled incessantly, but she was used to skipping meals, so it wasn't a major concern.

A woman from the 'camp' approached her. "Hello."

Kelechi studied the woman. She was a small woman, shorter than Kelechi and wore a big smile. Her hair was neatly woven, drawing her face and highlighting her brown color. In another life, she might be considered pretty, but with her collarbones peeking out from her low-cut blouse and thin arms, she looked like an egg with limbs. A very pregnant egg.

"My name is Ifeoma," she said, thrusting out her hand for a shake.

So far, she was the only person who'd spoken to Kelechi like a human being, and it felt inappropriate to snub her, which wasn't the best idea if Kelechi hoped to extract information from her. Still, Kelechi couldn't bring herself to touch Ifeoma because she wanted to avoid germs. Instead, she raised her right palm to her mouth to cover a fake yawn then said, "Hello."

"Come, let us get back to camp."

Kelechi looked back at the compound, hoping to find something she missed, but everything was as she'd first seen it. The only difference was that another person displayed her naked self on the stage on the guise of bathing.

"Where's camp?"

"Over there," Ifeoma said, pointing at the canopy.

"But-"

"That's all you get unless you want to stay out here in the sun all day."

She was right, but not entirely. Kelechi would go to camp with her only because she couldn't possibly stay under the sun. However, that was not all she could get, as she'd surely leave as soon as she negotiated her release.

***

When you thought people couldn't go any lower, they always proved you wrong. The campers welcomed her with shouts that could wake the dead while quarreling over a bucket of water. The exchange was funny in a disgusting way.

"Na my turn to bath today," a lady who Kelechi sized to be in her early twenties said.

"I don't have the energy to argue with you. Hand over the bucket," said a second woman who looked about thirty.

"Madam, abeg I no get time for this rubbish. Two days ago, you baff my turn, yesterday you baff your own join, now you want do am again. Me no go gree you today!"

The younger woman stormed off with the tiny bucket in hand, only to return shortly thereafter, her face fallen and feet dragging. With her hunched shoulders and hanging dress, she looked worse than pathetic. "The water don finish," she announced.

Kelechi didn't understand what their argument was about until Ifeoma explained. Apparently, bathing was rationed. Each person was limited to a tiny bucket of water every other day.

"I can't follow such a rule," she told Ifeoma. "I have to have my bath twice a day or nothing will do." Kelechi ignored Ifeoma's smile. A smile that said, 'We've all been there'. However, Ifeoma had yet to understand they were nowhere of the same category. Kelechi was the woman who always got her way because she worked for it. Her time in their miserable camp decreased by the hour.

Even with the fruitlessness of the young woman to score a bucket of water, the other was far from done.

"The Bible said, 'no peace for the wicked.' You want to bite the fingers that fed you and expect my God to sit still and watch? No way!"

Kelechi expected the lady to challenge the woman, but she ignored her and instead went to a space in the shade and sit. The older woman followed her. Kelechi concluded that the older woman was the perfect example of a troublemaker.

"You ingrate. I feed, clothe, and shelter you, and this is how you repay me?" the older woman said.

"Madam no start o, this no be for house," the girl answered.

"Are you warning me?" Madness entered woman's eyes, which had grown so huge it was a miracle their sockets held them. She pulled off the scarf on her head and tied it around the waistline of her skirt which kept falling below her waist and she had been holding up and folding every few seconds.

From the brand logos on her clothes, Kelechi could tell that she saw money. Even her exposed weave was of fine quality natural hair. Even with all her seeming affluence, Kelechi feared she was about to get into a catfight.

"Chinyere leave that thing," the lady retorted.

"Do I blame you? You're now calling me by my name, and why wouldn't you? We eat the same thing, after all. If not for you, I would have been in the States with my family by now. Children of the devil, this is why they say you should never put a goat and yam together!"

The journalist part of Kelechi sensed a story and willed her legs to walk as close as she could get to them to ensure she didn't miss a line, yet careful not to be caught in-between. Everyone under the shed was now interested in their argument, urging them on with a suggestive 'what happened' hoping they'd tell, even Kelechi.

The madness caught up with the young woman. She stood to face her opponent, dwarfing the older woman. "So, after hearing that, you still put them together, disobedient child. When this yam told you what your goat of a husband was doing to her, what did you say?"

"How dare y-"

"Shut up! You ruined my life long ago. I begged you to send me home, but you refused, instead urging me to keep all the horrible things your husband did to me every night to myself. I will never forgive you, and the blood of my unborn child which you took me to abort leading to this horrible kidnap will hunt you all the days of your miserable life."

The young woman was sobbing, tears flowing down her chocolate-colored face like raindrops trickling down a windshield. Though Kelechi felt bad for her, she didn't dismiss her stupidity. She could have reported the man to the authorities. People in Kelechi's field clamored for such scandal, especially since the man was apparently rich.

At the pause of the women's quarrel, the campers' tongues let loose. Everyone seemed to have something to say, which they felt was more important than what their neighbors had to say, forcing them to raise their voices. Soon, it became market chatter. With the majority blaming the woman, she felt the need to defend herself and hence threw herself on the lady.

Hands got lost in hair as they scratched, pulled, and bit each other. They rolled around the semi-circle the campers had formed around them.

"Chinyere, stop it!" Ifeoma went to separate the fighting women.

"Ifeoma, you don't want to get tangled in this," a middle-aged man said, pulling the pregnant woman away from the brawl.

"But you know what will happen to them!" Ifeoma struggled to free herself from his grasp.

"They are aware of what will happen."

Chinyere tried to deliver a blow to the girl, but she ducked, and the fist caught Ifeoma on the side of her stomach. She yelped and clutched her belly. As she lost balance and fell forward,

Kelechi feared Ifeoma's stomach would burst and moved out of the way to avoid being splashed. Kelechi had never gotten over the childhood theory that pregnant tummies were like inflated balloons and as the belly grew, the thinner the balloon. A theory that was given to them as children to ensure they were extra mindful with expectant mothers, even though now, she knew better, that theory had shaped her. The guy took the opportunity to whisk Ifeoma out.

Kelechi's eardrums shook in protest as a large boom reverberated even to her soul. Her head ached to the point she thought her brain would rupture. Upon hearing the blast threatening to render her deaf, her mind refused to function past the ringing in her ears. Kelechi never knew silence could be so deafening, disturbed only by the soundless thunder playing jazz music deep within her soul. She registered everyone rushing to embrace the ground. Their movement was as strange as the sight her gaze couldn't free itself from.

A disturbance brought her back to the present. Her ears still rang, and her brain throbbed, but it finally interpreted the scene.

"Are you okay?" Ifeoma asked. She still held her stomach.

Was Kelechi supposed to be okay when people were being butchered in cold blood before her very eyes? Nevertheless, courtesy won over and she nodded.

She smiled faintly, letting it vanish almost immediately. "I'm sorry you had to witness this."

The editor in Kelechi demanded the full story, even though she would not get to report it, she felt she deserved to know how they were all going to die, "Where are they taking her?"

Ifeoma shrugged and said, "You came through the other side of the compound. You saw."

Kelechi felt the bile rise in her throat and swallowed severally to keep it down. She wished she hadn't asked. Kelechi forced herself to look at the girl who was filled with life just a minute ago, now sprawled on the floor at an odd angle, her left arm mostly torn from her shoulder, exposing the bone and still gushing blood, even as she twitched.

Kelechi clutched her stomach but yelped in surprise as her palm rested on something warm, sleek, and slimy. She shouldn't have looked, but she did and yelled out her lungs. From her chest down was covered blood!

"Come, let's get you cleaned up."

Blood and other particles she didn't care to dwell on had splatted on her. Kelechi couldn't believe that she was experiencing these barbaric acts. She allowed Ifeoma to lead her towards the platform, too disgusted to think further than that. Kelechi was always sure about how she felt about any situations, but as she held the blouse pinched from her body with her thumb and forefinger, Kelechi couldn't decide exactly what she was angry about; the guard for remorselessly wasting a life, or the wasted life wasting her expensive blouse in the process. Couldn't she have been left out of their whole drama? I yearned for a scapegoat to blame for the misfortune that began yesterday. But the truth was that even though she could blame the Uber driver for arriving late, her neighbor for delaying her, even the government for not fixing the road which directly connected to her avenue, Kelechi knew that no one was to blame, it was just an unfortunate reality.

"Take it off," Ifeoma said.

It took a while for Kelechi's brain to process what she'd said. "You mean I should take my shirt off before everyone?"

"Yes, unless you will be comfortable wearing the bloodstained shirt all day, though the good news is that it will dry in no time."

"What will I wear while you wash it?"

"Well, I can't wash it."

Kelechi realized then how brazen she must have sounded. Ifeoma was not her employee that she'd expect to assist her in all things, but even if she were, it would be rude to make her wash Kelechi's clothes with such a gigantic tummy.

Ifeoma noticed her discomfort. "No, it not that. I wouldn't mind washing it for you, but there's no water."

"What are you saying? I am expected to walk around naked and dirty?"

"Here." Ifeoma removed the black material she tied round her head and handed it to Kelechi. "It's my blouse. I got too big, so they gave me this shirt, now I'm glad I kept it."

The woman seemed kind enough, still, Kelechi couldn't imagine herself wearing another person's cloth, especially since there was no evidence that it was washed.

At Kelechi's hesitance, she added, "Don't worry, I'll find a way to wash yours so you won't have to wear it longer than necessary."

"Thank you." Kelechi gave it to her. Ifeoma was sensitive and, better still, understanding. At least with her, Kelechi didn't have to explain or make excuses for herself. The blouse was too big, but it was better than walking around in a bra, or worse, a dead girl's bloodstained shirt.

Ifeoma's breathing seemed faster and shorter than before, and Kelechi figured she must be tired from all that drama. "Let's head back to camp," Ifeoma suggested, almost in a pant.

Two guards dragged the dead girl's body toward the block. Kelechi ran over to them, careful not to look at the corpse. "I asked to see the leader, but I haven't seen him yet."

They continued their way and Kelechi feared they'd ignore her. Then one responded, "Why are you looking for the leader?"

"To negotiate for my release."

He looked at his colleague, then back at Kelechi. "Why do you think he'd grant your request?"

"Is the purpose for every abduction not ransom?" Ifeoma arrived and placed a restraining hand on her shoulder, but Kelechi shrugged her off. She had an anthem that worked: doing nothing changes nothing. Ifeoma may be comfortable living here for the rest of her life, but Kelechi had important things to do for herself and the world. "Listen, I'm tired of this whole stupidity. Name the price because I don't want to stay with these miserable people any longer. And please, cut down on the killing, else you'll run out of people to collect ransom for."

The guard hefted his end of the dead body and he and his partner continued. *Why were they so reluctant to negotiate?* They probably wanted to scare everyone to the point where prisoners would gladly pay substantial amounts to be released. They shouldn't have tried so hard; Kelechi had had enough traumas from the past two days to last a lifetime.

"Go back, when your time comes, you will be attended to," he said as he set the body down to knock on one of the identical doors on the wall-building.

"Their stubbornness makes no sense to me," she said to Ifeoma.

The expectant mother laughed. "Prayers are about to start. Do you want to participate?"

"How will that help?"

"Everyone is always so eager to join, but not you. You're different."

Finally, someone noticed. Kelechi gave a half-smile. "You're not joining?"

"No."

"Why?"

"I feel it's a selfish kind of prayer. They pretend to pray for everyone's release, but everyone is just interested in theirs. I believe this is the time to pray for others more than yourself. Pray for God to reveal Himself to the kidnappers, not for the Holy Ghost's fire to blast them to oblivion."

Kelechi shook her head. She believed this was personal and prayers, if necessary, should be treated as such. The killers were hardened. Invoking the Holy Ghost's fire on them would show them mercy, which they didn't deserve. At this point, abyss would serve.

Two different guards exited the building, and one halted to look at Kelechi for a couple of seconds. But when the other continued towards the camp, he followed.

Ifeoma held Kelechi back. "Don't go."

As they watched, one guard grabbed a female camper by the hair and the other prowled to a male crawling a pitiful retreat and snatched him by the ankle. "What will happen to them?"

"What happened to the fighters?" she asked.

"Wait, shooting hostages is not a first?" Even as Kelechi spoke it, she knew the answer, yet seeing the pregnant woman shake her head confirming her fear was more than Kelechi could handle. If they were worth over two million each, what was the point of killing them? Unless... "What will they do with you people?"

"*All* of us, you mean? You're coming from the other side of the fence. You saw."

Kelechi turned away from Ifeoma and gave in to the puke rising from the pit of her stomach, again. Though this time, nothing came out.

FOUR

KELECHI HAD HELD onto the hope that the kidnap was a mere ransom demand case. She had even plotted the angle from which she'd report it. Though her bank account and probably those of her family members might be emptied, she would live, work and start saving again. However, that would not be the case now; she was going to die, butchered like a fowl, and no one would ever hear the story. Yes, a missing person report would be filed, but that would just be another headline that would last all of one day.

Ifeoma tapped her back, whispering soothing words. What she was hoping to achieve with that was beyond Kelechi's understanding. Knowing that she was doomed to die in this godforsaken place was enough to rob kindness from anyone. Kelechi hated her unnecessary compassion.

"Why?" Kelechi asked.

"Politics."

"With this many people? What exactly do they do with them?"

"Trust me, you don't want to know." With the hint in her comment, Kelechi bent over and continued her business, and when it was over, she didn't argue as Ifeoma led her to the shade.

***

Kelechi swatted at a fly; they seemed to be in abundant supply and wouldn't leave her alone. She wasn't hungry, but she was thirsty. The bucket of drinking water the guard had brought had been fought over and she was only able to get a cup because Ifeoma gave up hers for her. Only after Kelechi had quenched her thirst did she remember that Ifeoma was pregnant and therefore needed it more.

"It's fine," she had said when Kelechi apologized.

The pungent stench was unbearable. The sun was so hot that it might as well have been inside the tarpaulin. Kelechi's joints ached. She needed a proper bed, in a proper room with proper air conditioning. She was dying for fresh air, decent sleep, and above all, a long cool bath.

"Madam, follow me," A militant ordered. But as Kelechi attempted standing, he aimed his rifle at her. "Stand and I'll shoot you!"

Kelechi was confused. Hadn't he just asked her to follow him? That was soon rectified as the expectant mother, sparing a look of regret for the confused lady, followed him out. Kelechi felt betrayed.

In a little while, Ifeoma returned and had the nerve to lower herself beside Kelechi.

"What's up?" she asked. She was looking fresh and fed.

"Apart from, say, hunger, dehydration, and in a few hours maybe, death?" Kelechi couldn't hide the hurt from her face.

"Just take it a day at a time."

Kelechi scowled. "Easy for you to say. You've probably never gone hungry."

"Calm down. We're all hungry—"

"Who the hell are you to tell me what to do? Going around getting special treatment while the rest of us rot! Maybe you even offered sex as a payment seeing as your tummy is this big and all..." The hot sting on her cheeks caused tears to blind her temporarily. *How dare she slap me?*

In an icy tone, Ifeoma snapped, "Who are you to make baseless accusations against me? You want to know why I get special treatments, you ask, but I'll never standby and let you run your tongue about my child!"

Ifeoma's reaction was something Kelechi didn't care for, and even though she was right, Kelechi wanted to let her know there were boundaries, but Ifeoma's next words, though spoken with calm was the most horrifying story Kelechi ever heard.

"I have been here for over five months. Five months of watching everyone I was abducted with getting butchered. They kill four people per day, and more if anyone falls sick, fights or a rebellion breaks out. For five months I watched people walk to the other side of the wall every day, knowing what would happen, and knowing that each new day brought me closer to the executioner. You want to know the reason why attention is given to me. It is the same reason why I am still alive, and that reason is this baby in my womb. This is my first pregnancy in twelve years of otherwise blissful marriage. As soon as they found out that I was with child, they kept me. They all are excited about my baby; I don't know why. They took me in now to feed me my daily dose of a foul-smelling herb. When I refuse, they put my feet in hot water because they don't want to bodily harm me for the sake of the child."

Kelechi looked down at her feet, which looked very pasty. Apparently, she had refused a time too many.

"I'm sorry."

Ifeoma smiled. Her strength was humbling. Kelechi couldn't imagine what would be going on behind her friendly exterior.

"Don't be. I'm only sorry for this child," She said, "I prayed and fasted for an opportunity to be a mother. My husband and I were very excited and really prepared for his arrival, I can't bear the thought of bringing him into this, for these people—"

"Hey, take it easy," Kelechi urged. Ifeoma's breath was short as she spoke. Kelechi thought it was the anger, but looking at Ifeoma, she noted how ashen her face looked, how tightly her fingers curled around her skirt, she seemed focused on something.

"I think my time is here." She gasped, clutched at her belly, and true to her words, water snaked from under her towards Kelechi. Ordinarily, she would be disgusted, but at that moment, all that mattered was Ifeoma. Kelechi helped her up and led her over the bodies in a quest to find a bigger space. Nothing mattered, not even the gun pointed at her by a guard who had just come over.

"Where you dey go? Oya sidon for there before I blast you go hell!" he yelled.

"She's in labor!" Kelechi screamed.

"The baby don dey come?" he asked excitedly.

Apparently, that was more exciting than getting Kelechi's head blown off. "Yes. Do you have a midwife around?"

"You go born am na," he said.

"I'm not a nurse. I know nothing of childbirth!"

"No be woman you be? Na to just born baby I ask. Do am jare!"

The guard was a boy really, and Kelechi knew exactly the word for him, but then, he wasn't worth her time, attention, and least of all, words, so she ignored him. "Please, who can help deliver the baby?" she asked. Kelechi looked around, but the majority seemed dazed, and others were what you could only call curious. "Okay, who has any experience with birth?" this time she focused on the women in the group.

"I have given birth twice, but I didn't know what happened past the pain," a middle-aged woman said.

Two young boys came forward. "I don't know what to do, but I'm willing to help," one of them said.

Kelechi took in a deep breath, she couldn't let herself be overwhelmed, two lives were at stake, there was no room for fear. She had watched a clip of a birthing, done biology in secondary school, all these were not enough, but they were all she had. "Okay, I need hot water, clean towels, a brand-new razor-blade and blanket to make her comfortable."

The militant spoke in a native tongue into his transmitter and smiled, exposing brown crooked teeth, Kelechi wanted to puke again.

"Someone go bring am, una go stay here do the business."

Kelechi's eyes widened in disbelief. "Here? It's sunny and unhygienic!"

He nodded, "Eh, sunny and unhygi—whatever. Na where you go stay be that."

Kelechi wanted to argue, wanted to ask if that was how he was birthed, but the woman's tug at her shirt, and her moans, spared him from her lectures, and her from his gun.

"I think the baby can't wai..."

Kelechi guided the soon-to-be mother a couple of feet away from the other captives, under the vigilant eye of the guard, and then lowered her. A boy not older than thirteen brought a bag containing two wrappers, one towel, and an unopened razor blade.

"Where's the hot water?" she asked.

The boy looked at the guard, then back at her and shrugged. "E never boil."

Kelechi inhaled deeply, hearing Ifeoma's moans get louder. "I need more clean towels."

"Towel don finish," the boy said, already retreating.

Kelechi wondered briefly what he was doing there; if he was kidnapped or sired by one of the militants. But she had no time to dwell on that. She focused on making Ifeoma as comfortable as she could. Her pain was coming faster and longer, she couldn't hold the screams in anymore. One of the boys used the towel to soak up the sweat that glistened on her face and shoulders, while the other fussed over her, being more in the way than helping.

Ifeoma raised and spread her legs, giving Kelechi a close view of what lay hidden. It was a struggle for her not to retch. She wondered the last time the woman had shaved. Probably before she was abducted, or way before that, because the hairs between her legs were thick enough to cover any other thing one would have seen. Kelechi looked around at the hostages. She wished one of the women would step forward and do the dirty job. All eyes were focused on them, but no one was coming close.

Goosebump after goosebump raked her skin as she hacked off chunks and chunks of dark tangled pubic hair damped by what Kelechi refused to think about. This was the dirtiest job she'd ever done in her life. Even though the blade was sharp, her shaky hands caused her to cut into the skin with each scrape, causing droplets of blood to coat her palms and the area she worked.

When the area was marginally clear, she stood and found one the boys holding a bowl of water waiting for her. It was a good thing. Kelechi scrubbed and rubbed, yet no amount to washing made her hands feel like they were hers. She doubted she could ever eat with them again, or even have them touch her skin.

"It..." Ifeoma panted as she tried to talk, but another scream tore from her lips. Kelechi looked down between her legs, at the greatest miracle of all.

For Kelechi everything happened in a blur, but the moment of moments was when a tiny, warm, bloody bundle slipped into her outstretched arms, and she had to brace herself, so as not to drop the baby. It was a baby boy, and he was the most beautiful thing on earth.

The baby began to wail. Something about his warm red body and sleek hair caused a feeling to blossom in Kelechi's heart, spreading warmth through her body. A cheer sounded through the camp and Kelechi turned, face all smiley, to present her gift to them, but killers flanked her, all looking jubilant. She hadn't noticed them arrive. Her chest constricted in pain. She held the baby tight, stepping back from them. "No!" Tears blurred her vision as a guard reached for the baby.

"You're done now. Hand him over."

Everywhere turned dark and her head felt light. The slap a guard gave to her loosened a couple of her teeth. Then he grabbed the baby, and she gave him up, for fear that they would tear the baby if she held on. It was all so unfair.

"Oya, e don do, go back now."

"I have to help her." She squatted to help clean the mess of birth, but the first guard grabbed her.

"That's not necessary," said a voice she could never forget. The man who had shot her driver in cold blood.

Kelechi froze, but only for a moment as he took the baby from the guard. He was a very tall and handsome man. Kelechi couldn't believe that she would ever use the word handsome to describe an albino, but the man facing her was appallingly so.

"What are you going to do with him?" she asked, nodding towards the bundle in his arms.

"That's not your business." He conversed with his fellows in that native tongue used earlier, and they all nodded in understanding. Next thing, two of them carried the new mother and headed towards the block of doors, while he, escorted by four of his men, carried the baby towards another door.

Kelechi couldn't say what was in store for the baby, but she very well knew the fate of the new mother.

She wished there was something she could do to save both, but even as she tugged on the sleeves of the last of the guards, she knew it was futile. Still, trying was the least she could do.

"Name any amount for their freedom," she said, swiping at the tears blurring her vision.

"Girl, you never learn? No one here wants your money."

"But there must be something I can do. Every man has a price."

He looked at her so long she feared he may decide to take her to the other side, but then shook his head and left, taking the soiled towels with him.

Defeated, she went back to the canopy but couldn't sit. Had Ifeoma been there, she'd have smiled, told her it'd be fine, and offer her soft but powerful peace, reassurance, and friendship.

None of the hostages had done anything. Even though she knew that nothing they did would have stopped the inevitable, Kelechi felt repulsed, too repulsed to share the shed with them. She took her soiled shirt which Ifeoma had meant to wash and sat at the birthing site.

FIVE

THE NIGHT WAS the most disturbed of Kelechi's life yet. She woke up drenched in sweat too many times that she lost count. The nightmares that woke her were so horrible and felt so real that they had her too scared to close her lids. Yet, she'd sleep again only to be awoken by more incubi, each one more terrifying than the last.

The morning was even more treacherous, starting with scorching heat even before 8 am, to thunderstorms before noon. Then an even angrier sun, so hot that steam rose from the hostages' damp clothes.

The upside was that everyone got to drink enough water, though it was too bad they didn't have anything to collect more for reserve. The campers also got to have their baths and Kelechi even washed and wore her own shirt. She tied Ifeoma's blouse on her head, partly to use it to hold up her hair from her face, but mostly because she didn't want to lose what tiny piece of Ifeoma that she had.

A couple of men wheeled in a large food warmer in a barrow, and bags of water in another.

"Oya, two people should come and serve the food," the shorter one ordered. As soon as he set the barrow down, he brought out a game from his back pocket and was soon lost in its world.

The other stood and supervised, though you could tell he'd rather be someplace else. He hopped from one foot to the other as he directed, as though the ground was on fire.

The young woman passed the food as another dished grub to Kelechi, handing her a watered-down version of what looked like soup. The soup was filled with greens, half-cooked vegetables. Kelechi wondered if the soup was barely cooked in consideration of their health, or because the cook wasn't bothered.

"No, thank you," Kelechi said, thrusting the paper plate back. But her stomach chose that moment to growl.

The girl smiled, withdrawing the hand she already stretched to retrieve the plate. "Eat, at least let's stay alive for as long as we can."

Kelechi nodded, already too embarrassed to insist. The girl was right, 'where there's life, there's hope.' Kelechi scooped a handful of greens and shoved into her mouth, not even bothered about washing her hands. Germs had become the least of her worries.

After the meal, Kelechi volunteered to take the trash to the fence where it'd be easy for the men to carry. The game guy whose nose was still lost in the tiny screen gave no objections. Kelechi was sure he was relieved as the other guy had gone back the moment the hostages settled down to eat.

On a good day, Kelechi wouldn't have bothered, but she noticed the man from yesterday at the door. He was on sentry duty, and it may be her last opportunity to get a word to him without his colleagues lurking around.

As Kelechi approached, she could see the sentry's dark pupils at the corner of his eyes, watching her. Though he looked at Kelechi with rapt attention, his face was stoic. Whatever he had in mind was concealed behind thinned lips and a blank face.

"Good afternoon," Kelechi said tentatively. The man continued looking ahead, not betraying any emotion. Kelechi lowered the barrow and turned back the way she came. There was no use trying too hard. If he would not help her, she'd find another way. Either way, she would not die a miserable hostage.

Under the tarpaulin canopy where the hostages were, a little girl had an asthmatic attack. Some campers encouraged her to breathe, others ignored her. Kelechi learned from Ifeoma that the girl and her mother were kidnapped on their way to the hospital. The little girl's mother was killed the day they arrived at camp.

She turned back to the guard; her shoulders squared. She would try her best before giving up on him.

"Hello mister," she said. When his face remained stoic, snuffing out the last of Kelechi's hope with it. Just then she thought she saw a slight nod of his head. Kelechi wasn't sure, but she decided to try again. First, she looked back to make sure Mr. Gamer remained a few paces away. "Please I don't want to die here, can you help me?"

Again, he ignored her, even after she rephrased and asked several times. Kelechi took her cue from the arrival of Mr. Gamer and went back to camp.

What was I expecting? He had told me yesterday that there was no hope or help for us.

Now, she reconciled herself with the fact that no one in the camp would help her. It was time to think of another way. Whatever happens, she would not be a helpless victim.

The captives found a way to entertain themselves in the camp. They were about two dozen, so they divided themselves into four groups. The first told stories, the second lectured on history, the third decided that they needed prayers and led them through hours of firing supplications to God. If He was somewhere like they all hoped, then it'll be impossible for Him not to have heard. Kelechi watched the display in awe. Some were praying in gibberish, spittle flying out of their mouths as they revved like a bad generator. Some held the wall, pushing and invoking thunder and lightning to shatter it. One man kept throwing himself against the fence, declaring that as he was pushing, so should the host of angels. It was like a madhouse, everyone praying in forms that Kelechi wouldn't believe possible was she not an eyewitness.

After that session, no one felt like tainting the moment with more silly entertainments, hence everyone took to themselves, some singing, others having a quiet time. Still, there were those who felt they had a special relationship with God, so their prayers continued. The most annoying, for Kelechi, was the wall pushing man. He would run a few feet back, then run with an energy none of them should have and slam himself against the wall. Kelechi felt like dragging him back by his collar.

Deep in her heart, Kelechi hoped, but she was realistic. No one knew where they were. No one knew about this fortress, and there was no escape means. The only savior they had was money, and the kidnappers weren't interested in it. They were doomed — at least until she was able to figure out a way. But where was the guarantee that she'd be alive long enough to find a way? Kelechi stood and left the canopy. She walked around the part of the camp where the hostages went, then farther. The plan was to know the kidnappers' reaction when she wandered too far. The place was fenced, but none of the campers, even Ifeoma had attempted to go near the west fence.

The knowledge that she was hours, maybe days away from death brought back the gloom caused by the fear of the unknown. Kelechi's mind wandered to a million places; if she died here, where would she spend her eternity? Has she been too obnoxious? Had she hurt people with her attitude? What was her relationship with her family? Did she show enough care? Of course, she loved them, but did she make them feel it? What would she be remembered for?

What was her relationship with God, and what exactly happened to her Faith?

Kelechi was raised in a Christian family, and she was even a chorister in her school's fellowship. Kelechi could not pinpoint when she began backsliding, but she remembered church being in her way; days when she needed to attend some party in other to report, when she had a meeting or interview to prepare, when she needed to go on trips, or when she was just simply drained from a hectic week. When Kelechi wasn't looking, church became a leisure activity, until it became her past. Or maybe her eyes were open the whole time.

Kelechi thought she was probably the Jonah of the other kidnapped people's prayer. She still had enough knowledge of the Bible to remember. Even if it were so, just like Jonah, she would sit the storm out with them, or until they find her out.

Kelechi felt a shiver run down her spine and a feeling stop her in her tracks. It was the feelings she got when someone watched her. She looked back in the direction of the camp, but she could've been nonexistent for all they cared. She turned in a slow circle until her eyes fell on the man by the door. The guard. He looked at her so intently that Kelechi was surprised no tears fell. On looking closer, Kelechi realized that he attempted to inform her something. It was the same man whose help she had asked for previously, so she hurried towards him like a beacon.

"At midnight, guards will change. We will be less conspicuous then. Tell no one, not even a soul. Both our lives depend on it." He began speaking as soon as Kelechi snuck within earshot, and then turned back before she even got to him. Still he didn't reach his spot before a door opened. Both men exchanged nods and the newcomer disappeared into another door.

As hard as Kelechi looked at the man, he didn't spare her a glance. One wondered if he spoke at all, or maybe her imagination controlled her.

But Kelechi knew she heard him clearly. At that moment, her biggest challenge was to keep the smile off her face till midnight.

"By midnight I will be free again," Kelechi told herself to make sure she wasn't dreaming.

"I'm not going to die here," she said again, and this time, she couldn't help but jump up and pump her fist in the air.

"What are we celebrating?"

Kelechi turned so fast she tripped. Facing her were two men; the one that'd almost caught her and the guard earlier, and the second driver who brought her— the albino. The first smiled like the Cheshire cat, while the latter had a frown that gave him the look of King Kong.

Kelechi glanced at the guard who had promised to help her, but he peered straight ahead. Only his stiffness betrayed how tense he really was. *Could my actions make escape impossible?* Kelechi balked at the thought. She had to make things better. "Yeah," she said, her voice quaking. She cleared her throat, and when she spoke again, her voice was firmer. "My kidnapping, what else?" She rolled her eyes then turned and left. She felt their eyes on her as she walked to the edge of the canopy, and the knowledge that they watched her was the only thing that kept her from collapsing. Then they walked past, observing the hostages for a few minutes, and then drug the asthmatic girl with them. She held onto another hostage, a young man, screaming and sending spittle flying out of her mouth all over the young man she held like a vice. The man tried to pry her fingers off himself, but she wouldn't let go. The kidnappers didn't relent. They struck her at the back of her neck, then dragged her limp body with them.

Kelechi prayed they bought her act; or else she may be the next to be dragged out.

She spent the rest of the evening fretting for what may or may not happen. Kelechi didn't know which she feared most; the men finding out the plan, or the plan failing.

To avoid a sticky situation, she stayed away from the other hostages; it wouldn't do develop attachment with any when she was going to leave them in a few hours. But the major reason was to avoid a slip, though those were completely out of character for her, but five days in hell can make one lose oneself.

Kelechi settled in the open, away from the others as darkness took over. It was very chilly, as was the usual in whichever hemisphere they were held, but she needed to make sure that during her exit, she would not be noticed.

The moon hid behind the clouds, hence cutting off any shade of light and all chances of reading her watch face. Kelechi lay face up, listening for movements. She didn't need her watch, or the cockcrow to tell her when midnight came and went.

Kelechi wondered if he had been found out, or maybe he changed his mind. But more than anything, she wondered if she hadn't imagined the whole thing all on her own. God knows she'd read enough stories that her mind sometimes found it difficult to pick fiction from factual.

The daily circle was broken by mid-morning when loud activities from the other side of the fence kept everyone tense. It sounded like those over there where preparing for World War III. There were screams, shots, the sound of car engines, and more wailing. The Watch had left his post after breakfast as was usual, however, no one else replaced him. It was not strange as it's happened a few times in the past- security wasn't a worry at this side of the fence.

After a while, doors opened at random, admitting guards first, then an endless stream of new captives. Some were arguing, some crying, some nonchalant. But they all had something in common; Kelechi's pity. They probably believed that there was a way out. There were more kids too, ranging from infants to adolescents. And just like their age differences, they wore different expressions, from excitement to confusion to total terror. Kelechi pitied them all.

Among the guards that brought them in was Kelechi's supposed savior. She watched him, waiting for a reaction. When he got to her, he went past her, neither sparing her a look or a word. Kelechi decided that he was either having fun at her expense, or she was a dreamer. One thing was sure for Kelechi would never entertain him. She ignored him. He wasn't going to save her after all, or maybe the word was 'couldn't'. Kelechi would never know.

A set of twin girls were having a field day with their tongue, wagging them at whoever came across or spoke to them. On a good day Kelechi would have been irritated at such manners, but today, she was just sad for them. They were pretty and tall with an ebony colored skin worth dying for. From their English you could tell they were not from the middle class; they spoke broken English like they invented the tongue, yet their outfits were those of the higher class. Kelechi encountered enough of their kind regularly to know that they were runs girls. The type that slept with affluent men for money.

"Move joor, who dey follow you talk?" one kidnapper said, pushing one of the twins.

Like a swarm of angry bees both pounced on him, and within seconds, he was lost amid flying limps. The girls fought like tigers. Soon more of the new captives joined.

The commotion brought mixed reactions; awe from Kelechi and other hostages, amusement from some of the kidnappers, anger from the others, and fear from the new arrivals.

It was easy to predict exactly how this was going to end, and even before Kelechi saw the albino reach for his gun, she ran back to escape any repeat performance, or worse, getting caught in whatever was about to take place. She moved far away from the crowd.

A tap on her shoulder sent her reeling backward, tripping on her own feet as a result. The guard caught her wrist just before she hit the ground. "Hurry! go through any door, it'll lead you to the other side, keep running until you're outside, and even then, don't stop. I'm right behind you."

Kelechi didn't hesitate, she made her way towards the farthest doors to the great wall. It was longer, but it'd keep her out of peripheral views. For anyone to see her, they had to turn. Her heart rate spiked and the urge to run spun her head. She prayed the girls would keep them occupied a little longer.

Kelechi pushed the door as soon as she reached it, determined that nothing would take her back having come this far, at least not alive.

The room she found myself in was nothing like the one she had passed through when she was brought in. This one was moderately furnished, but Kelechi didn't stay to pleasure her eyes. He ran for the opposite door, which was mercifully unlocked, pushed past it and made her way towards the huge gate.

A few bodies lay unmoving in the blazing sun where Kelechi had been made to spend the night the first day, but she didn't wait around long enough to check whether they were dead or alive. As she approached the gate, Kelechi feared that it may be locked. If so, it would be back to square one for her. She knew she would be taken straight to the chopping block. Getting nearer, Kelechi saw the padlock securing the metal and her heartbeat came to a stop. Chills ran over her even when her insides felt like they were on fire. She'd never get out. On their own, her legs slowed while her mind worked. Going back was out of the question for her. Chances were her reemergence would not go unnoticed. Moreover, she wasn't willing to go back after coming this far.

A hand grabbed Kelechi's, causing a scream to tear through her throat.

SIX

"SHUSH, YOU'LL BRING them right to us!"

The man who had promised to help Kelechi pulled her along with him as their legs flew up one after the other behind them. Kelechi hoped he had a key.

He proved to have something better. He left her hand but only to turn the padlock. The iron had been carefully placed to look locked, while all the while it had been open!

Finally, they were surrounded by greens which at first were sparse but soon became so thick that they had to push themselves through its abundance. Still, they didn't slow. Kelechi's thighs ached from the scissoring, her muscles protested, but her mind was stronger. They kept running until dizziness threatened to overtake Kelechi.

"We can't stop," he said, when Kelechi began to slack.

"I-" Kelechi couldn't get the words out. Her heart drummed against her chest, blood deafened her hearing, and she panted like a thirsty deer. She seized the moment and stopped, then shook her head, hoping he'd understand the unspoken words.

"There's a lake a mile and a half east of here, let's get there at least, so we can have water to drink."

Kelechi didn't think she could raise her leg ever again, but the prospect of water was a strong motivator. He held her up, his arm behind her, lending her enough support to make the trek with him.

Kelechi was beyond thankful when she heard the gentle roar to the river not long after.

"We ran farther than I calculated."

"Thank God. Is it safe for drinking?"

"Yes."

The tributary was so clear that Kelechi saw the smooth pebbles carpeting it. She let go of his support and ran right into it. After a few moments, she turned back to see him walking away down the bank.

"Wait, you can't leave me here!" Kelechi was already running out of the water. He wouldn't rescue her just to leave her here, or would he?

"I wasn't trying to leave you. Rest while you can, we have a long trek ahead of us."

His words were reasonable, especially considering that her calves ached, and her feet were bruised and bleeding from cuts. Kelechi sat on a rock protruding from the smooth soil of the shore and rubbed her feet.

"Wait, where are you going?" The thought occurred to Kelechi that he really had no reason to wait for her. There was nothing holding him back from walking on without turning back.

"I have something further down," he said.

"Let me come with you." He gave no rejection or acceptance, just continued walking, so Kelechi hopped up, wincing as the heels of her feet protested.

She shouldn't have bothered. He turned towards the bushes and stopped in front of a tree. When he stood, he slung his newest companion, a backpack, over his shoulders.

Kelechi had a lot of questions, but as she watched him make his way back, she bit them back. Now wasn't the time to risk annoying him. If Kelechi rubbed him the wrong way, then he may really leave her.

The man said nothing to her while they huddled to wait out the rain. She tried getting him to begin moving, but he wouldn't budge. If Kelechi knew her way, she would have been long gone.

It began raining almost as soon as he returned carrying the backpack. The rain in this clime gave no warnings; one minute it'll be so sunny you'd think you'll melt, the next, the wind will start howling like a lion, the clouds will turn gray, and the downpour would begin.

Instead of braving the rain like Kelechi had told him, reasoning that if their disappearance was noted, it'd be hard for their chasers to follow. He had been adamant in his refusal, countering her reasoning with his own. 'Our steps would be easy to follow if we walk in the rain.'

Kelechi deduced three things about him; he said little, he wouldn't listen to her proven wise council, and most importantly, like her, he was running from his men.

Kelechi itched to milk him for news, but since he'd decided not to talk to her, she wasn't going to beg his attention.

"Can we go now?" she asked when he made no move to resume their escape even after the rain stopped and the weather warmed.

"The ground's still muddy," he objected.

It was enough crap to eat from anyone in one day, still, Kelechi took a deep breath and tried again, giving him the respect for rescuing her. "It will soon be dusk; I'd rather put in more miles between us and the kidnappers before the journey becomes impossible."

"Girl, you don't understand a thing. It is more dangerous to make a slip. These men are thorough, and you don't want to know what will happen if you get caught."

Kelechi's nose flared and her breathing became heavy. She didn't know which was more insulting and annoying; him calling her a girl or him accusing her of mediocre. She opened her mouth to answer back and in doing so, wash him clean with her words, but then decided he wasn't worth it, after all, he was part of the very group she ran from. Who knows, he might even have a deadlier plan than those she'd escaped from. Kelechi turned and left him.

"Girl, where do you think you're going?" he asked, running behind her. Kelechi wouldn't have spared him a moment but for the restraining hand he placed on her shoulder.

First, she rearranged her facial expression, making it as flat as possible, then turned to him, making the action deliberate, hoping it sent the message she was about to give. "Call me a girl one more time, and I'll make sure you don't live to tell the tale." It was a bluff, she didn't have enough strength to deliver a blow that'll kill a rat, but she hoped that his flinch meant that he bought the act. She continued, "Why should I trust or listen to you? Let's not forget that the men I'm running from are your men." Kelechi may not have been sure the first time, but this time, she clearly saw him throw his head back. Whether in hurt or the surprise that she'd talk back to him, Kelechi didn't know and at that moment, didn't care.

Now that she began, Kelechi decided to let it all out. "You wouldn't know how it feels to be held prisoner, but worse, you wouldn't understand what it felt like to live every moment knowing it may be your last. The counting of the seconds knowing you'll soon be dead and unable to so anything about it. You can never comprehend what it is like to take food and water from the very people who will soon end your life. You don't know what it's like watching them take human after human and knowing full well the fate awaiting them. The fate that draws nearer to you with each breath.

"I don't expect you'd understand because they're *your* men after all." The tears fell freely from her face and she wasn't even conscious of it. The unsolicited memory of Ifeoma and her newborn, the maid and her madam, the man and then the child from yesterday, the twins a few hours ago, and indeed all the kidnapped rushed through her mind like she watched a slideshow. Kelechi swiped at the tears trying triply hard to swipe the images from her mind. She was lucky she got out, but she would only be truly saved when she escaped this damned forest and back to her life. However, true freedom would only be achieved when she rid herself of those horrid memories. Kelechi focused instead on the face of the man whose name she still didn't know. She savored every bit of pain that his usual stoic expression couldn't hide. She didn't mind that he was in pain. In fact, she didn't care that he was in pain or what may be causing it. Whatever it was, Kelechi hoped it haunted him to his grave.

She couldn't resist one last jab. "I'd rather keep moving than risk them catching me. Know why? Because like you said, I can't imagine my fate if they caught me, and you'd know better. You're them after all."

Kelechi turned and headed into the unknown. She knew he wasn't following her because there were no footfalls, not that she expected him to. Kelechi had had enough of both him and his men. She didn't need him. She would just walk until she finds a road or house. How hard could that be?

Kelechi's mind still boiled in anger. Her chest felt so full that she feared it would burst. Who brought someone out of the lion's den only to keep them within said lion's reach? But more importantly, who killed when he could get money to do otherwise? From the last batch she met when she was kidnapped, they could get immeasurable wealth, adding that to the new arrivals which were about twenty or so people, then she can't possibly tell what they'd do with all the money. They will be rich enough to buy Nigeria. But no, they had to kill all those people, plus the ones they'd killed in the past.

Then after coming this far, one nincompoop who had no respect for women wanted her to risk going back to square zero for doing nothing, she would keep walking until she either fell dead or met human life.

"It's too dark to know where we're headed. Let's rest today and try to get an early start tomorrow."

Kelechi's heart skipped several beats at the voice. She didn't know he still followed her or hear him behind her. And true to his words, it had become pitch dark, and she'd missed that because she was lost in the world that existed in her pain and anger.

"You can be angry with me all you want, and rightly so, still should use your he- sorry. Still you should listen to me. Once we get lost, even I can't help. We need to set our emotions aside and make it through this first, after which we never have to see each other again."

It was difficult for Kelechi because her ego was hurt, but she halted. He was right in the sentence he didn't complete. She really needed to use her head, though she was glad that he cut himself off. She didn't know where she was or where she should be going. She needed him, and she was glad he used plural to define them.

"Fine," she said, turning towards him.

The wind kicked in, chilling her to the point of shivering even though she doubled her shirt with Ifeoma's. The man explained why they couldn't light a fire, though Kelechi didn't mind. She welcomed the discomfort of the weather. It brought a distraction from her thoughts. She was glad for the after-rain sun that dried her off because she couldn't envisage being in that weather in wet clothes.

"Here," he said, thrusting a wrap in her hand.

He rummaged the pack for so long that Kelechi bit her tongue to stop her from complaining. As she unfolded the wrapped leaves, Kelechi hoped for his sake that it was worth it, or else, she wouldn't be held accountable for what her mouth might say.

It was. It was roasted meat whose aroma caused her stomach to rumble in appreciation. Kelechi broke off a bit, but as it got to her lips, she threw it down.

"What's wrong?" he asked, the arm that dug in the pack flew out as if bitten by a snake.

"This is human meat, isn't it?" Kelechi asked, revulsion churning her stomach.

By his huff, she imagined him rolling his eyes, then his arm delved back into the pack and continued.

It annoyed Kelechi that he'd ignore her. She wished she could bash his head against a tree. The man had a knack for being annoying, and Kelechi hated that she needed him. "I said, is this human meat?" she threw the rest at him for emphasis.

"First, lady, I have gotten to my limit of patience and understanding with you. You are rude, insufferable, ungrateful, and senseless…"

"All I asked for was the type of meat, I didn't ask for this insult, man!"

"Mind you, you didn't ask. You accused…"

"I vividly recall saying, 'I said, I this human meat?' that is a question."

"Don't cut me off while I'm talking, learn some manners. And using 'I said' is very different from using 'I asked' moreover, in your first comment, you began with saying 'this is human meat', not exactly the way a question is phrased."

He had the upper hand and she didn't want to concede defeat, so she changed tracks. "So, is it human meat or not?"

"What made you think that I'd eat human beings?" he raised the trophy he'd finally found from the pack- another wrapped leave. "What do I look like to you?"

"A kidnapper who hack people in pieces and bag them." Not because of his sudden sharp inhale, Kelechi really didn't mean to say that. Unfortunately, words said couldn't be unsaid. He stood and walked away. She listened to his footfalls until she couldn't hear them again. He was right, she was senseless. She had just driven away the only person who knew how to get her out of this forest.

SEVEN

WITH HIS ABSENCE, the presence of the night grew. Kelechi began taking note of the shadows that shifted and changed. It was so quiet that it seemed as if the elements were watching and stalking her. Even the breeze had given way and not a leaf moved. The only sound that kept her company was the palpitation of her own heart.

Kelechi laid down using his pack for a pillow, though it felt nothing like soft. She clenched her lids shut willing sleep to overtake her. Everything will be better in the morning.

But sleep rejected her too. Kelechi listened for sounds even in the distant, but nothing came. It felt like she was alone in the universe.

To distract herself, she thought about work; how she'd sell the story of her kidnap. It didn't need padding. It was unbelievable enough to sell and people loved a good tragic story. All she needed was to come up with a punch line and a dramatic headline. She wondered how Alice coped in her absence. Kelechi thought of all the pending contracts for review. She worried what Alice may be turning her baby into. Thankfully, in a matter of hours, she'd be back to clean up any mess Alice's incompetence may be causing.

The good thing from this whole charade was that it'd keep her company at the top for a long time.

Thinking of the company was good for her mind. The next thing Kelechi knew was something shaking her foot.

"Wake up!"

The sound seemed to be coming from a dream. It was probably her roommate, Laide, in school; Laide usually shook Kelechi's right leg whenever she wanted to wake Kelechi up. Kelechi knew she should save her some frustration and get up, and they probably were about to miss a lecture, but she couldn't. Kelechi ached all over her body like a pride of lions used her to play basketball.

"Aww," Kelechi protested as something cold splashed upon her face. "It hasn't gotten- "she couldn't finish her sentence as her eyes opened to stare into hard ones.

"It's later than I planned, get yourself up and let's go."

Kelechi didn't argue, didn't even want to. She took his offered arm and pulled up, waited for him to zip and back his bag, then followed him out.

On second thought, she retraced her steps for the discarded meat. The dark brown chunk sat on the bare grass, yet Kelechi took it, feasting on it as she tailed him.

"Thank you for coming back for me," she said when at last they took a lunch break. This time, his search provided dried bread.

He paused in his hunt for his own loaf and eyed Kelechi for a second, then resumed, not saying anything.

"And also, for the meat, and this." She held up the half-eaten bread.

This time, he didn't pause, he just gave her a "hmmm."

"Also, I'm sorry for what I said last night about …"

"You sure have a mouthful today. Listen, I understand how you feel about me. I would have felt worse than that about you if the tables were turned, you don't need to pretend or lie. I'm cool with that. And I came back for you because I was heading out anyway, it wouldn't cost me anything, no big deal. We can make this journey without speaking to each other, that way, feelings would not be hurt, or boundaries crossed."

He zipped his bag and sat back, leaning on the large tree they sat under, and closed his eyes.

He wasn't entirely honest with her. Kelechi had seen his prints all day. He had probably walked all night, heading out of the forest, before turning back for her. She knew that he would be faster on his own. What's more, he'd given up his food for her. The second search yielded nothing which was why he laid back. He was a gentleman.

"Here," she said, holding out the remaining half of the bread for him.

He eyed it for a moment then closed his eyes, ignoring the bread.

"Really, take it. Even you need to eat. I can't have you die off on me in starvation."

"You are sure you're full?"

She wasn't, but it didn't matter. "Yes."

He took the bread and in no time, he finished and washed it down with water from the river.

"What's your name?"

He took so long she gave up on his answer before his reply came. "Ekanem."

"Calabar," Kelechi said. She had long since learned to place people by their names.

"Yes."

"My name is Adanna." Kelechi felt she needed to guard her privacy from him. Even then, she wasn't telling a lie. She also answers Adanna.

"You're Igbo and the first daughter in your family?"

"Yes. You know about your country." Kelechi was pleased that he understood tribes not his.

"Ada is popular, you don't need much knowledge to decipher that." The silence continued, but this time, it was uneasy. Then he spoke again, "I've never really taken Ada as a name, more like a title. All Ada also has personal names. It's OK if you don't want to tell me yours."

In another time and place, she would have taken up the debate. As he said, Ada is the title for every firstborn female, though not limited to them. If she engaged him, she knew exactly how the argument would flow. He would say it was unreasonable to name a girl Ada since the girl will still answer to that regardless. Kelechi would argue that since she was an Ada nonetheless, it made no difference, then he'd counter that first sons do not bear their title 'opara' as a name. It was one argument that she had lost over and over while in school.

Determined to preclude further hard feelings between them, Kelechi changed the topic. "You're not hard enough to be a killer. I wonder what you were doing with those men." She meant every word. He had had enough opportunities to harm her had he been a bad person. When they make it out, he may then demand to be compensated for his trouble, but Kelechi had already decided that whatever price he asked would be fair enough, provided it was monetary.

For the average person, the line she delivered would have been perfect to get them talking, but he continued to stare into the distance. "Why were you with them?" she asked more directly.

"I was misled."

"By who?"

"A friend's friend."

"How?"

"We were broke and jobless, my friend and I, so we went to one of his guys who promised to show us the way to quick money. I knew it'd be dangerous, but after spending months of borrowing and running from debtors, I was prepared to do anything."

"And he brought you two here?"

"Not immediately. At first, he had us run errands for him, minor things that set me at ease, and he paid profligately for the littlest things."

"What kind of things?"

"They range from doing his shopping to slipping a powder in a girl's cup. But soon, I was able to offset my bills, paid my debts with interest, and started a business for my younger sister and my mother. He was an answered prayer to me."

Kelechi could imagine what it was like for him. She herself came from a middle-class home, still, she was never hopeless. She had however dealt with his kind before. They were the poor useless sobs who you could send to rattle up a party so you could get news. You could walk all over them and they'll still lick your feet if you asked. For money, anything was worth it.

"What happened to the girls you drugged?"

"I didn't know or cared to ask. I assumed that when he was done sleeping with them, he'd settle them handsomely and everyone will walk away satisfied. I didn't take him seriously when he joked about his being celibate. Judging from the number of girls my friend and I drove in; I had no reason to. I even thought he was a pedophile."

Kelechi's breath caught in her throat as the meaning of his words dawned on her. She was afraid of his answer, still, she asked, "You brought kids to him too?"

He rubbed his hands together, then rubbed his face as if attempting to wipe the reality of what he's done. "Yes. We'd give them money and send them to go and greet him or send them to buy stuff and deliver to the gentleman in the car. The tricks we used for children were endless and he paid even more outrageously for each."

Kelechi drew back, putting more than an arm's length between them. "And so, you brought in more seeing as delivering kids were lucrative." She could not hide the accusation in her voice. No matter how broke they were, giving out children was inexcusable. Even though he hadn't known that they were being killed, delivering them to be raped was just as bad. "Did you for once stop to think of the future of those children? The trauma and the state of their mental health? Of even their parents? Didn't it occur to you that they could've been your child or that of your precious sister who is even now living off their blood?"

"Yes, I did stop to think, but that was at first, in no time I lost count how many I delivered, and I stopped thinking or caring. I recited my mantra every time I was sent on an errand, 'this is the world for you. It is kill or be killed'. But you don't need to imagine the different horrible things that should happen to me, or the million ways fitting of me to die."

Kelechi was halted that he read her mind and the pause had her looking at him, really looking. No one could be in more pain than he. She may be mad at him, but he was even more so at himself. All the while he spoke, he managed to twist his fingers into an awkward looking knot. Kelechi thought of offering him relieve with a hug, but the memories of countless folks who entered her office over the years to report missing persons prevented her.

"Once we make it out, I will surrender myself to soldiers, tell them what I know what I've done in detail, and hope they make things right. I will pay for my crimes, but first, we need to make it out alive."

Kelechi did a mental one to ten count to keep her calm. He at least, planned to make things right, while all along, she thought of different ways to use the situation for the furtherance of her business. Kelechi had not stopped for a moment to consider how she could help the other captives. She'd proven again how selfish she was. It was an itchy realization, one she wished to move away from.

"How did he bring you to this place?"

He looked at Kelechi for a long time, then shook his head. "Understand this, I'm not proud of what I have done, and I do not like to talk about this. But I have this strange feeling. I need to tell someone, in case—" he chewed on his lower lip.

"Well, in case what?"

"In case — so it doesn't die with me."

Kelechi thought for a minute. She didn't know what he was talking about, so she prompted him to continue his story. "How did you end up here?"

He blew out air from his lips, then sat up and hugged his knees as though he was in pain. "One day, the man called us and asked if we were ready to enter the next level. Of course, we were, so he set a date and time for us to gather. He encouraged us to tie up any loose ends because we would be staying for a while and didn't want anyone filing a missing person report. I didn't dare question where we were going, not wanting to aggravate him into changing his mind."

"What did you tell your family?"

Ekanem stared into the distance, reliving another day. "I told them that the man I worked with wanted me to go on a trip with him, and I didn't know when we'd return."

"Did they buy it?"

"Except my brother. He insisted to go to his house with me to pray for a safe journey. He is a pastor."

The irony wasn't lost to Kelechi. Two brothers, one a pastor, the other, a kidnapper. "How did you handle him?"

"I didn't do much. I just told him that the man was a Witness and wouldn't appreciate it and the effort might cost me the connection I was building. My sisters took it from there, not wanting to lose the sudden income source as well."

"And your parents?"

"My father is late, and my mom never takes sides in siblings' squabble. She just waited for whoever won, then ensured that peace was restored."

"I take it you won?"

"With my sisters supporting me, Pastor Paul didn't stand a chance. And so, I went with my friend to our rendezvous point, to find three more guys added to us."

"He had more recruits?" Kelechi's stomach churned at the thought of how many more lost lives that meant.

"Not necessarily. I would have known if he had others working for him. I think his friend sent them."

"You know this friend?"

He gave a faint smile. "You question like a reporter."

Kelechi smiled too. It then occurred to her that she could ask his permission to publish his story. "Actually, I am."

"Interesting. Which media?"

"Phoenix Reviews."

"I submitted my CV there once."

"Oh. Our hiring standard is pretty high." Kelechi didn't mean to sound obnoxious, and she was glad he wasn't offended.

He smiled. "I am a first-class graduate from Unical."

"What? Then why were you without a job? First class is a guarantee for a job!"

At that, he laughed for a long time, then drew near to Kelechi and placed his hand on her shoulder in a patronizing manner and said, "Dear, your company rejected me as well."

"Your CV never made it to my desk then. There's no way I'd pass up a first-class degree certificate."

"What are you, the chief editor?"

Kelechi thought Ekanem had a knack for looking down on her, so she seized the opportunity to set him straight. "Yes, and even better, I am the director."

"Phoenix Reviews is directed by Mrs. Elizabeth Obasi," he said.

Kelechi heard the smirk in his voice before it appeared on his face. "Yes, but that's in the past tense. I've had that position for 3 years."

"Her daughter, Kelechi Obasi, took over."

"You're impressively abreast with news of our company. Anyway, I share the same surname with her, that doesn't make me her daughter."

"You said your name is Adanna, I guess the cat is out of the bad now."

He laid back on the tree and closed his eyes. She expected a reaction, but he was gifted at being unpredictable. Not that Kelechi expected more from someone who'd delivered children for money.

Then he stood up, "We've rested enough, let's move."

"How much longer till we get out of this godforsaken bush?"

"My dear, the journey has only just started."

EIGHT

THANKFULLY THE WEATHER was clear disarming Ekanem with reasons to make them walk in the thorny shades of the bush. However, with it came heat that caused them to drink water every few miles. Kelechi was grateful that they walked along the river, even the few times that elements cut them out, they still found their way back to the stream.

Kelechi and Ekanem learned how to coexist without the constant threat of punching or leaving each other. They discussed impersonal topics like politics, football and culture. He expressed his delight at Kelechi's abilities to discuss intelligently. Apparently, he still didn't believe that she was who she said she was. Kelechi wasn't offended, in fact, she appreciated his honesty and the logic in his views, he was unbiased, and he was smart. The kind of workers Kelechi would pay any amount to have.

"You never finished your story," she said, as they walked side by side under the early morning warmth. It was their third night in the forest and Kelechi knew from experience that the warmth would soon turn to scorching heat.

"Huh?" he asked, his face taking on that stoic expression that had disappeared from his face since the day before.

Kelechi was sorry she brought it back, yet she wanted to hear the whole story.

"How the man brought you and your friend in," she clarified. Kelechi knew he had understood the first time. He gave her the opportunity to let it go. However, she didn't want a friendship, she wanted a story.

"He drove us all to another house, where we met others too, about a dozen or so of them?"

"In the same town?"

"No, it took us at least a day's driving to get there?"

"At least? How can you not know?"

"Because, princess, we were drugged. He had five of us drink some stuff and as we drove past familiar terrain, I felt so nauseous that it was a chore sitting straight."

Probably the same stuff you fed your victims. Now, what do they say about being fed in the same spoon you feed others with? Kelechi thought, and would have said so except it may break the newfound camaraderie, and worse, end the story.

"Time and distance lost meaning to me until I woke in a room filled with a dozen young men. A couple slept at awkward postures; the rest sat tensed. I think they were as wound up thinking of how the day would change their lives as I was. Only a couple of boys, I think in their late teens chattered excitedly. They didn't speak any Nigerian tongue, I doubted we were even in the country."

"I noted you made no reference of females, and there were none in the camp."

"Indeed, it never occurred to me, but there was never a female. Probably another of their female phobia. Once you become part of the gang, you must never have a sexual relationship with a woman. It is one of their strongest rules."

"Yeah, I noticed," Kelechi said looking away in embarrassment as she recalled the humiliation of the guard looking at her like she was some rotten piece of meat.

"Anyway, we were given a long talk on the 1%, loyalty, brotherhood, secrecy, and whatnot. Then they asked who had a change of heart. I was planning to tell Mr. A Plus as soon as I saw him again that I wanted out, so I saw no reason not to raise my hand. I asked Koffi, that's my friend, he too was having doubts, so we raised our hands along with four others. All five of them, Koffi and the other four, were shot right where they stood, then in a very flat tone, the orator told us that there was no way out, not after coming this far."

"The man that shot them was the albino?"

"No, his name is Ngijabe Namiti and he makes Mr. Kimaiyo, that is the albino, look like a saint."

"Wait, you raised your hand too, why weren't you killed?"

"God saved me." It was the last thing Kelechi expected to hear and she didn't know how to respond, thankfully, she didn't have to. He continued, "I started to raise my hand with the rest when my left eye began to itch, so I brought it down to scratch the offending area. When I was done, I began lifting my hand again, but saw Ngijabe Namiti reach for his waist. I was saved because God wants to use me to expose them."

"So, you followed them all this while waiting for an opportunity to escape?"

"The plan was to get information about all their ranks, but the longer I stayed, the deeper and grosser it got. They have three tiers people of my rank allowed to know information; the importers, the keepers, and the exporters. The importers brought in victims and the keepers minded them."

"I'm guessing the exporters transport the body parts?" Kelechi had wondered about that since she was held.

"I'm guessing the same thing. The two teenagers plus one of the guys that rode with us were chosen as exporters, then while we were taken to be transported to our posts, they were kept back for their own prepping. The most I know about them is that like importers, they could live outside the camp."

"Keepers are not?"

"A keeper has to earn his freedom to live outside the camp and return for his shifts."

"How long have you been here?"

"It's my second month. I wish I'd left earlier."

"Did you get information on the other ranks?"

"No. being secretive is a requirement, and everyone wishes to climb the ladder. When I report myself, the authorities would do that."

Kelechi doubted that. She suspected the killers would have members in places of public authority, but she kept her reservations to herself. "Why did you save me? We both know that you would have been ten times faster on your own."

"As they dragged the new mother out, I knew I couldn't stay any longer, evidence or not, so I made up my mind to leave. Then you came begging to pay any amount, not for your freedom, but that of total strangers. I had never seen such selflessness, it brought tears to my heart. At that moment, it became clear what God wanted me to do. Remember the scripture 'blessed are the selfless…pure in heart'."

What Kelechi did then had been purely impulsive. Though she wished she could have saved them but placing them above her own safety wasn't something she was known to do. But it felt good hearing such a report about herself. Over the years she had built the reputation of not being nice or considerate, and she felt it suited her just fine provided she did my job. But maybe being kind occasionally wouldn't hurt after all.

"Also, I'm hoping that one if not both of us makes it out alive and bring rescue to those still living," he said

Kelechi sent a silent wish to be the lucky one to make it alive, then caught herself and instead prayed that they both survived.

"I've watched lives taken every day for two months, my best friend was shot right beside me, I've seen humans beaten like cows, and all the while I'd been helpless. Even if this is the last thing I did, I will make sure that I and everyone else involved will answer for those lives here on earth first."

Kelechi thought of the feeling she had had when the fighting woman's blood had drenched her. She thought of what it felt like to watch the driver die right in front of her, she thought of how she felt that first day, seeing the girl first beheaded, then chopped. Then she weighed it against what it must have felt like to watch your friend die right beside you. "I am sorry for your friend," she said.

"I made him raise his hand, he wouldn't have otherwise. Ngijabe Namiti shot him like a worthless paper target. His blood splashed on my face, an accusation, even in death, that I was the reason he was dead. I was the one who wanted out. I should have been dead, and him alive."

Kelechi stepped into his path, forcing him to halt. She touched his knuckles, tout against the straps of this backpack. The face looking over her head, refusing to catch her eyes, was that of a man in deep anguish. A man haunted by himself. Kelechi wanted to tell him that it was alright, after all, he was making things right. She wanted to reassure him that talking his friend out of the life they were living was noble, and there was no way he could have known that they had no choice. Kelechi wanted to tell him that she understood. But she knew words would never be enough to comfort him.

She offered the only comfort she knew, realizing only after she put her arms around him that in giving him comfort, she was also giving herself some of it. And she hadn't realized that she needed it as much as he.

He hesitated a moment, then rested his head on her shoulder, accepting the hug.

"He was an only son, and all he wanted to do was make life better for his family. He worked the hardest even as a child. His dream was to make enough money to build a big house, then get married and have six children. He never did any of those because of me."

"Shush, it is OK. God allowed it to happen, so who are we to question Him?" It was the right words because he nodded, then sniffed into her shoulder. Kelechi wasn't repulsed, instead, she rubbed his arm, his pack in the way of getting access to his back, and Kelechi felt rubbing his head was too intimate.

They remained that way for a while, giving him enough time to get himself together, then he tore away from her like he just discovered she was a contagious septicity. "Run!"

Kelechi didn't have time to process his scream. She heard the words, but they made no sense. He grabbed her hand and rocketed into the bush.

With one hand supporting the bag, and the other clasping hers, he didn't have a third to push the thick bushes and low branches away. In effect, they tore at them and slapped at their faces.

Kelechi pulled her hand, ready to demand what he was doing, but his vice-like grip didn't bulge. Then she heard it.

A booming sound ricocheted through the forest, sending birds to flight and sense to Kelechi's brain. They found them, just like Ekanem suspected they would.

They kept running, legs flying behind them. Then Ekanem stopped. "Go, run and don't turn back."

"Not without you," Kelechi said, meaning it.

"Fool, you still have a chance. Take it and use it for good."

"So, do you. Remember the Lord kept you for a purpose. You have to live to be of use to Him!"

"I now know why I was urged to take you with me. The task is yours after all. Escape, so that you can save millions of lives. It's too late for me now."

Kelechi looked down at him clutching his stomach. Blood streamed down from an ugly hole. She felt paralyzed. She didn't know what to do or say. She couldn't believe that Ekanem was also going to die on her.

He knelt, struggling to breathe. "Stay away — river — find   you — trust — one — informant — hut — help — tell him Ekanem — pro — ."

"No Ekanem, you can't die, no, not like this please." He lost blood fast and talking was becoming harder. He mouthed 'go' for Kelechi, then made a failure of an attempt at laughter.

The footsteps grew louder reminding Kelechi that if she wanted a shot at making it out alive, she needed to move. Yet she couldn't, she held Ekanem's hand wishing she had the ability to turn back time.

"Save yourself Kelechi, save them, and tell our stories," he clenched his hand on hers, and breathed his last.

Kelechi wanted to scream until her lungs busted, she wanted to give each of the kidnappers a slow horrible death, yet her feet on their own moved the rest of her body.

She couldn't run, because if she did, it'd give up her position, so she hid in a gulley and closed her eyes, allowing the pain of one more loss drown me. Ekanem said God was in control so Kelechi figured if that was true, then He'll be open to making a deal.

She sent out her terms to Him; *hide me from these evil men,* she said, *I couldn't care if they shoot me right now, but I guess You'd care if You want me to do whatever.* Then she laid down leaving God to make His decision.

NINE

THE MEN SURROUNDED Kelechi, their shots echoing through the tall trees and thick overgrown grasses.

She wasn't hidden, at least not fully. The slope at which she hid barely covered her head.

She listened for and gauged their distance from their footfalls, the dry twigs and fallen branches making them impossible to conceal.

Kelechi knew when they got to Ekanem; whoever it was that got to him first shouted, "I don see am, he don die!"

"I needed him alive," a man whose voice sounded like Mr. Kimaiyo's growled.

"Where's the one he was with?" another asked.

"E get another one?" the first guy, an obvious illiterate, asked.

"I think so, I'm not certain though."

"Spread, everyone. I want this place combed. If there is indeed another one, then they must be found. You, this is all on you, just pray no end is loose or it will not be the only."

Kelechi didn't know who he was threatening, but she could tell how whoever it was feeling.

One thing because apparent to Kelechi. They didn't really know of her disappearance. If she makes it out, no one will really bother her.

However, they were determined to search the length of the forest, meaning that she couldn't be safe where she was for longer.

Kelechi tried to get up and survey, checking how many men there were and weigh her chances of slipping by.

But as she raised her head, she was almost caught by a guard who approached her hideout. Her instinct was to make a run for it, but Kelechi crouched right down.

Her heart thumped against her chest, her palms sweaty, like the rest of her body.

The evening advanced, with the speed night fell in the forest, and the breeze which was getting stronger did little to help matters.

Kelechi sent out prayers to every god, and even one to Ekanem, enlisting their help in not being found.

It started to rain, or so she thought, until she looked up to see a man holding down his penis at her.

Kelechi took a moment to assimilate what was happening, then closed her eyes hoping that when she reopened them, the nightmare would be gone.

A few heartbeats later, she did, nothing changed. Kelechi wasn't horrified, she was numb of all feelings.

How was it possible that in all the vastness of the forest, the man chose to do his business on her head?

Kelechi considered pulling him by that idiotic part and yanking him down. She was going to die anyway, but the man just had to degrade her in all ways possible before doing the honors.

She looked up at his face again, the urine falling into her upturned nose. But he wasn't smiling; he wasn't even looking at her.

He had his face turned up too, his eyes closed, enjoying the moment. The moment of Kelechi's humiliation.

'Yeah right,' Kelechi thought, *'at least you die before me.'*

"Anyone there?" the albino called out.

"No," the man said, hurriedly zipping up.

Kelechi was just about to raise her hand to draw him by his penis, then his words sunk in. the idiot hadn't seen her.

As he walked away, Kelechi crouched still, like a statue, listening to their retreating footfalls. Even after then, she couldn't get up, she didn't have the courage to. It felt like someone lurked somewhere waiting for her to make her appearance.

The wind grew violent, making her position even more precarious. Finally, Kelechi stood, falling multiple times because her knees kept giving way until she succeeded.

She got out of the makeshift cave and surveyed her environment. All around her were trees, overgrown weeds, and more trees. Animals weren't moving about, at least not that she could see.

She ran back the direction where she had come from, or at least where she thought was the direction, hoping to see Ekanem. She needed to see him one last time, and give him a proper grave, or at least as proper as she could manage.

Kelechi kept running, pushing against the wind and the greens. There was no sign of him. Everywhere looked alike, and it got darker.

She tried to find her way back to the cave, but that too seemed to have been sucked into nonexistence.

Cold, tired, aching, hungry, and defeated, Kelechi sat against a gigantic tree and wept.

Once she let go of the dam, she couldn't stop it- didn't want to stop it. She sobbed for everything, from the decisions she took the morning of her kidnap, to her attitude way before that. She cried for the memories she left people with and the image she built of herself.

When the tears began to curb, Kelechi found new reasons to cry. She thought of the deaths, of the child and Ifeoma, and she wept even harder for Ekanem.

She needed to cry, not only because it gave her something to do, but also because it made her feel less alone.

Kelechi cried until tears refused to flow, still, she didn't stop until sleep enveloped her in its peaceful embrace. The sun filtering in through the thick roofs of the jungle alerted Kelechi that it was day.

She opened her eyes and wished she hadn't.

There was a yellow patterned snake coiled around her ankle.

Kelechi had been abused, insulted, and forced to eat trash. She had seen people die- killed and shot. She had taken more than she thought was her limit, yet she survived.

But seeing a snake, not just in person, but having it on her body was the most she could take. Kelechi felt her eyes roll up as she fainted.

When Kelechi came to, she looked down, and to her horror, the slithering beautiful monster was still where it was.

This time, she didn't faint, she acted. Kelechi screamed so loud that she was surprised her vocal cords didn't burst, all the while shaking the occupied limp.

In response, the snake uncoiled itself, drew it's head back with mouth open wide.

Kelechi knew what was about to happen, and the thought of that was so overwhelming that she passed out a second time.

The insistent bespattering of the rain on her face forced her back to consciousness. Kelechi was disgusted to see that the rhythmic movements of the water beating the dirt had sent them flying and messing her up even more.

She tried to get up, but a slight throb on her ankle had her sitting up with force as memories returned.

The snake was no longer there, but it did leave a souvenir: two punctures on her skin.

Dread immediately replaced all other emotions. After all, Kelechi wasn't going to die by the killers, but by a snake.

There were no chances of her getting to the hospital fast enough to save her life. An article she had edited several months ago for publishing explained that the victim of snakebite had at most thirty minutes to live after being envenomated. Kelechi had no idea how long the snake had bitten her for, but it wouldn't matter anyway. She didn't know how far away from civilization she was and even if she was close, she still didn't know her way out.

Kelechi became fully aware for the first time, how dangerous it was to be in the bush, without supplies and alone. And worst of all, without hope.

The fear of the crawling creature returning with backup got her to her feet. She tested her leg and breathed out in relief when she stood and took a few steps.

Kelechi was hungry, tired, bitten by a snake, and alone.

She felt like a speck of dust in the wilderness. Nothing in this place gave a damn who she was or her personality.

She walked and walked around in the forest with no destination in mind.

She saw a tree thick with sweet bright yellow fruits, one of the strange fruits they were fed in camp. Her stomach growled in remembrance and excitement, and her brain urged her to hurry towards it.

It was refreshing to finally be able to eat. It would be her first meal since Ekanem was killed.

It occurred to her that she had been up for over thirty minutes and still alive, moreover, the bite wound wasn't purple or blue like the article said it would. It was a dull red. Also, her mobility strengthened her suspicion.

she may have been bitten by a non-venomous snake.

Kelechi stuffed her mouth with the sweet and sour fruits, not minding that they weren't washed. Soon, her head began to feel lightheaded. She plucked a few more of the fruits and continued on her way.

The bite area was swollen, her mouth tasted foul and her stomach hurt. It was like the end was near for Kelechi, but the thought of dying in this forest and her body devoured by whatever lent a new strength to her.

Kelechi plunged on, then downwards until she met the ground.

In her current state, it would be fatal to lose consciousness, because she may never regain it, and the snake, or another or even another animal altogether might come for her.

Kelechi tried as hard as she could to keep her eyes open, but with each passing breath, it became more and more a chore.

She scrunched her eyes tight, then released them, only to find a pair of black eyes set in hollow sockets surrounded by shriveled skin swimming in her vision.

Kelechi tried to scramble away or scare whatever creature it was, but the effort only increased her migraine, until the world around her disappeared.

TEN

KELECHI FELT HER feet fly over uneven plateau sending shingles and whatnots flying behind her. The wind swooshed past her ears, still she was neither tired nor out of breath.

Shots were everywhere, forming a background rhythm for the forest around her. Everything was alive, from the footsteps approaching her from all directions to the animals running for cover.

If only they knew that the men weren't after them, but the bundle in her arms.

"Stop, give over the child and we'll let you live."

She didn't need to look back to know who had spoken, it was Mr. Kimaiyo. She could tell the lies in his words. He would never let her live. But through his voice, she could tell that they were closing in even faster. She needed to up her speed if there was to be a chance of escaping.

As if in confirmation, the child squalled. Kelechi held him tighter, even as her legs added as much speed as was possible.

Then the sky darkened, making her hazy visual which was already a problem, to get even worse.

"Hand them the child." Kelechi heard Ifeoma's voice but couldn't tell the direction it was coming from. It was as if it came from within. "It's not worth it. Live to fight another day."

It was already difficult running for her life and adding the cumbersomeness of supporting a child who wouldn't stop squirming, further dimmed her chances. No one would say she hadn't tried, after all, it was the baby's mother who acknowledged that it wasn't worth it.

"Give us the child and you never have to worry about your life and welfare."

This time, she knew the voice belonged to Ngijabe Namiti. Though she had never seen or heard from him before, the convictions in her heart gave no room for doubts. She felt herself begin to slow.

"The child is mine, is he not? I'm telling you to give him up."

Something wasn't right, Ifeoma sounded a little too desperate. *She probably wanted to exchange her baby for herself too,'* Kelechi thought, *'and who'd blame her for that?*

"Don't stop!" came the frantic voice of Ekanem, "It's all a lie and they are all a lie. Ifeoma is dead, do the right thing. I know there is goodness in you. Prove it to them!"

Ekanem was right, Ifeoma was dead.

"But you didn't see me die. I've changed my mind, bring back my child, it's time for his nursing."

Kelechi heard the fear in her voice clearly this time. For some reason, Ifeoma was scared. Kelechi picked up speed she didn't know she had and sped ahead until her legs became weak and failed to support her. Then she felt herself plunging to meet the ground.

She felt the pain then; it was all over her body, from her pounding skull to her aching feet.

She opened her eyes and saw the devil's older brother staring at her.

❋❋❋

The man kept swimming in and out of her vision. One second he would be clear, the next he would double or triple, then totally blurry like he was fading.

"Here, drink."

She felt something cool against her lips and moved her head in an attempt to avoid it, the effort making her neck and head pay for it.

The man held her neck pressing the cup harder. "Is fever, is break. You drink, you better."

It took a moment to figure out what the man had just said, still, it made no sense- nothing did.

She drank the concoction and immediately regretted it. it was the foulest tasting thing possible. Her mind went to Ifeoma, was this the kind of horror she was made to ingest?

The old man who looked more like an ape urged her on, "more good, less bad, you die."

Kelechi pressed her mouth tight while holding her breath. The thing didn't just taste bad, it smelt worse and she'd rather die than take another sip, as it was, she wished she had her toothbrush and paste.

The effect of whatever had been mixed there was a million times better than it smelt or tasted. She felt the throb in her head fade steadily like sand through open palms. Her throat hurt less too, giving way to hunger.

Her stomach quivered, she wondered the last time she'd eaten, she wondered how long she had been in the muddy hut and who the man was. She could have asked, except that it wouldn't matter anyway. For now, she was glad she was alive.

The man brought out a calabash from behind him and attempted scooping the dark contents into her mouth. She began to understand what was happening. The man found and saved her, still, it didn't justify his mannerlessness.

"I didn't say I wanted to eat," she said, even though her treacherous stomach grumbled its protest.

"Medicine make you want food." He brought the contents of the spoon close to his lips to indicate what he was talking about when he spoke next. "Green cook with fine root, good for you."

Kelechi cringed at the thought of eating the grub the man held. Not only was it brown and unappetizing, but as the man spoke, she saw the spittle fly from his mouth and there was no way they would have escaped the scoop right before his lips.

The man was insistent. "Sweet, cook you special. Eat not die, not eat die."

Kelechi reasoned the man's words even more. She had been bitten by a snake and it was probably the man's food and medicine that kept her breathing her. But more than that, she needed his cooperation if she was ever going to find her way out.

She took the earthenware from him, still, there was no way she'd be expected to eat the scoop already in the spoon.

She threw down the contents of the spoon, then scooped another from the bowl. She hesitated at the spoon before her mouth, then granted it access Kelechi pushed the grub around her mouth with her tongue first, then began to masticate. She raised her eyebrows and she chewed. The food was a mix of vegetables with some fruits cooked in what she didn't know. It was the most delicious thing she had had in time immemorial.

With her level of starvation and the delightful taste of the food, she didn't stop until nothing remained.

"Please can I have more?" she asked.

But the man's face had become very hard making his eyes even smaller like they would escape deeper into their sockets. Kelechi had never seen the devil, but she wondered if she could tell him apart from the man staring hard at her.

"Drink your medicine," he ordered nodding at the remnant of the concoction.

Kelechi would have given him a piece of her mind. She had asked courteously after all. But three thoughts made her stick her tongue inside her cheek: one, with the way he looked at her, he may kill and bury if not eat her and no one will bat an eye; two, she needed him to survive. One day alone in the forest and she had kissed death. But the most important reason was that she was indeed very hungry.

She pinched her nose as she brought the bowl near her nose, whatever was inside didn't smell any better than it had the first time. However, she found that the taste improved, not enough to ask for more, but she didn't have to force it past her throat, especially since the effect was immediate.

She smiled at the man as she brought the plate down expecting well-deserved praise, instead, the man's countenance remained.

"Now, clean this place."

"What are you talking about? I am not a janitor." When the man continued to look at her, she decided that he probably didn't understand her. "No," she said.

"Yes, you clean. I give food and medicine and you pour food away on my home."

She looked well and saw that the look on the man's face was pain not anger and she let out a relieved breath she hadn't realized she was holding.

He was right anyway. No matter how the place looked, she had no right to disrespect it and him, after all, he saved her.

She got up from the mat, pleased to note that except for being sore, she was not in any real pain, not even from the bite wound.

The man left and returned almost immediately with a bucket and cloth and prepared to clean his house, Kelechi noticed that despite the size and quality, the hut was clean down to the red mud floor.

"I'll do that," she said, taking the cloth from him.

"You bite snake, you rest and heal. I clean."

"No, I made the mess, I'll clean it up."

The man lowered the bowl and went out, giving her privacy to survey.

The hut was empty, with few scatterings around. There were plastic bowls stacked against the wall with a kerosene stove and some pots stacked on one side of the wall. Then on the other, he had firewood, cutlasses and some farm tools.

Once done scrubbing the floor, she went out to see the man shucking corn. He didn't even raise his head as she lowered herself on the log he sat on.

"Feeling gooder?" he asked.

She bit her lip to keep from correcting him, and then said, "Yes, thank you."

He handed her an ear of corn and went back to his.

"What do I do with this?" she held up the corn for emphasis.

"You do this," he said shucking dramatically.

"I can't do that!" the wizened man gave her a look, one that wasn't threatening, but promising. "I mean, I'd love to help you, but I don't have a knife."

He handed her the black blade he had been using and resumed his task, this time using this thumbnail to loosen the grains.

Kelechi deliberated feigning ill to escape but decided otherwise. She would start making a positive impact in any life she came across, provided she made it out alive. She was here at this time, and she might as well leave a good memory.

"My name is Kelechi," she said for lack of what to say to the man. Small talk had never been her strong suit, and it was doubly worse since she and the old man didn't have a common ground.

"You call me Papa," the old man said.

"You have children?" Kelechi regretted her question the moment it left her lips. A man his age had to have children, but if he didn't, it'd be an awkward and sensitive topic. Plus, she didn't need someone subjecting her to a long tale of how unfairly life had treated him.

Fortunately, he did none. "Everyone call me papa."

Kelechi's heart soared so high she pressed hard and cut herself. There were other people which meant that she was very close to town and the old man could take her. She only had to double her efforts at being nice.

She noticed something she'd missed in her joy. The old man stopped and frowned at her, turning the gaze from her to the corn in her hands.

"Oh, never mind the cut, it's barely even a wound and I doubt I could get an infection from it." The man continued to look. "Sorry," she said.

She tried to shuck it like she'd seen the man do, but the blade kept finding its way to her palm, leaving little painful marks that didn't bleed. She let it clatter to the floor and mirrored the man. Her nail was an advantage. She rubbed two corns together, shaking them loose, then force them out using her thumb. Once she got started, however, she found it wasn't as hard as she thought, though in no time, she was covered in chaff and her palms became clammy.

"Papa, how far is the town?" she asked, mopping her forehead with the hem of her blouse.

"You walk, you reach one week."

"What! Aren't there vehicles?"

"No vehi- that thing you said."

"You walk one week to go to town?"

"I take motor."

Alice felt her heartbeat normalizing. "Motor as in car?"

"Yes. Motor go to town every week. It go today."

"I need to follow the car."

"Early morning it move, and it too cost."

"I don't mind paying any amount," Kelechi said, even though she heard the panic in her voice, she couldn't help herself."

"You get money?" the man's eyes were dancing at her. She nodded, bobbing her head up and down so fast that her vision spun.

"Show me."

She bit her lip, the man was right, and she needed his help once more.

"It's in my house, but I live very far. I promise to pay you back as soon as I get home."

When it became apparent that the man was not going to respond or take the bait, she re-strategized. "Will you take me when you're going to town?"

"I go one month; I go yesterday's yesterday."

"But I can't wait that long!" The man stopped and looked at her for a long time that she became uncomfortable, then went back to shucking the corn. "How do you get supplies then?"

"I don't get supplies."

He needed supplies regardless of how self-sufficient he was. "You need kerosene, matchsticks, spices, medicine and other things. Do you wait a month to buy those?"

"Oh, I get them from the village."

"There's a village?" as much as she tried not to get her hopes up, Kelechi felt her heart beating harder and faster, and nausea returned. She pressed her palm against her temple to keep it in check.

"Yes, it is not far, you go on leg in the morning, you reach afternoon."

"And by car?"

Papa looked at her as if she were daft, then said, "no car in the bush."

"Can you please take me there?" Kelechi dropped the empty husk and used the opportunity of free hands to rub her arms. She was cold even though her skin was warm. The headache returned, and with it, the dizziness.

"You sick. When you heal, I take you."

"No, I'm perfectly fine!" The young woman was petrified at the thought of wasting any more time when she was so close to freedom, and more so when the reason was herself.

She straightened her frame and clamped her teeth to control her shaking body. The traitor was between her and safety. She picked up two fresh pods and began shucking, this time it took a lot from her to apply the needed energy to the friction to shake the grains lose, but she did it anyway to prove to the old man that she was able to make the trek.

"You really in a hurry?"

"Yes, sir." Her teeth chattered as she spoke and no matter how hard she tried; she couldn't control it. Papa kept quiet and she took that as her cue to continue. "I really need to get out of this bush, wherever this is. I have a family that must be worried sick, a busi… well, I have been held against my will and really need to get out of this place. It is the only way I can feel safe again."

"I take you, but first, you need to drink more medicine and eat more food and sleep very well so you get power to walk. I old, I can't carry you."

"Thank you so much, sir!" It was all so surreal to Kelechi. She got up to greet him properly, but wobbled, toppling the grains she had collected in a basin. She bent to pick them but fell face first on the dirt.

"Go in, I bring food and medicine," Papa said, even he couldn't keep the laughter from his voice.

"No sir, I'll help you finish the corn."

"You help by going in, you stay you give me more work. We go early so we reach before sun is hot."

"Thank you, sir," she said, making her way back to the hut, holding the red mud wall for support.

As Kelechi lay and watched the old man walk around the room picking stuff, she calculated the possibility of not making it out after all.

With her luck in the past two weeks, she could almost associate the bitter taste in her mouth for the taste of failure.

She could turn out so sick that she would not be able to stand. The old man might just die, that is if she didn't die first, or he may just change his mind.

She thought of Ekanem, what he'd have said or what he'd have done. As had become customary whenever she thought of him, her chest constricted in pain, and tears welled up.

"You don't cry, I say we go very early before is day."

She nodded and took the bowl from the man, swallowing its contents to excuse her from not answering.

As the man continued looking at her, waiting to make sure no drop was left, something struck her. Ekanem had said something about an old man.

"Papa, are there other men living around?"

"In the village, plenty, in the bush I live alone. The dibias are far away, don't worry."

"No, it's not about that. There was this man, his name was Ekanem…" she saw his countenance change and knew she had hit the bulls-eye. "He said I should find you."

"He die," the old man said, standing up and out of her view. She couldn't see his face to gauge if it was good news or bad, but his voice said it all.

"I'm sorry, the bad men shot him."

He didn't respond but instead went out, abandoning his self-given duty of making sure she finished the herbal medicine. As she finished, Kelechi dropped the calabash and took up the second bowl. This time it was soup, though he didn't give her any swallow for it. Without a spoon to scoop, she drank it just like she swallowed the medicine.

Fed, warm and marginally safe, she lay back on the mat and slept, this time dreaming of home and freedom. She dreamt of walking down the aisle with Ekanem, but as he approached, the ground shook knocking the flowers from her hands.

The flowers turned out to be of midnight black and she looked back at her approaching groom but found Papa instead of Ekanem.

A loud slap stung the sleep from her eyes drawing tears. "Wake up girl!" Papa's face was close to hers, and as he spoke, the stench of his breath had her insides turning.

She understood he said that they had to leave early, and as eager as she was to set out, waking her in that manner was rude. She had only just started sleeping as it was.

But she held her peace, before noon, she'd be back to civilization, or at least close to it.

"Get up, hurry." The urgency in his voice mingled with the eagerness had her scrambling up, but as she was about to greet him, he put his palm over her mouth, with the other he pressed something in her hand.

Very low, Papa whispered to her, "They are here, run child and never come back. Don't make the same mistake Ekanem made, you cannot change the world."

"Papa come with me." The tears flowed free; she couldn't believe she brought her ill upon another person yet again.

"They don't harm me. They call me crazy old man. But they kill you if they find you and kill me for hide you. Now go, go only east, you find road the bridge. Cross it you enter village. You not stop but take car, I give you money. When you go to city you go home and forget everything."

"But Papa…"

"You not hear what I say. You run now or us two die. Now go!"

Papa practically pushed her out the door and only then did she see the real danger.

ELEVEN

THE BUSH ALL around was alive with light. Though the house itself was not yet engulfed in the brightness, but flashes swept all around like a spotlight.

"Go now!" Papa whispered again to her in urgency, slapping her back as he did, and the sting brought her out of the daze.

The kidnappers were really determined to kill her and everyone who attempted to help her.

She gave Papa a hug even through his stiffness, not minding at all that his dashiki was in dire need not for the dry cleaner, but blazing fire.

"Thank you, sir."

"No come back. Forget here and live life."

As she ran, she took extra care to avoid any beam, and more so to listen for footfalls other than her own. She had forgotten to leave behind Papa's slippers.

Time lost meaning to her as the wind howled in her ear. She may have been running for five minutes or five hours, she couldn't say, and she didn't care. What mattered was to put a reasonable distance between her and her assailants.

As her chest began to hurt and her head feel lighter, her legs grew heavy and her vision became unreliable. Twice she had ran into trees causing her head to protest even more.

Kelechi slowed to catch her breath and to give her ears a chance at hearing things other than her blood.

It was still pitch dark making her wonder when she had been made to take off.

Papa had told her to go east, and the moonless sky offered no help in aiding her.

She knew she was at a risk of getting lost again and couldn't decide which should take precedence — keeping a wide distance between them or securing the right direction.

Kelechi knew she had exerted herself too much already, and continuing wasn't an option, but she became petrified of sitting even for a moment.

She kept walking, even though it was a chore to put one foot before the other, but thoughts of Ekanem, Papa, and Ifeoma served as motivators. Their death shouldn't be in vain.

It was getting lighter with the dawn. And like the darkness, her strength ebbed. She tripped over her feet, inhaling dust as she hit the earth. She drew herself up to a fallen branch and sat on it, after checking to ascertain she didn't have any unwanted company.

The temperature rose, sucking the moisture off the elements, and her throat as well. She tried to swallow, but it seemed she had spent the last drop of energy in her.

The chill woke her. She couldn't tell how long she had been out, but the dark troposphere was as a result of rain clouds, not midnight.

The cold weather seemed to bring with it a new vitality. Her body still hurt, and when she stood, she was stiff in all the places that mattered. But with her newfound mobility, she chose to make progress.

First, she took a quick detour to an orange tree. When she got enough, and then some, then packed the fruits in her extra cloth which had been tied around her waist and holding it close to her bosom. She may not be able to control her life, but she was determined to do her part, no matter how little.

The rain started, but unlike usual, it was a mere drizzle. The light rain was unlike the thunderstorms which do a once over then paves the way for the sun. It kept falling, shrouding everywhere in mist and shadow.

Through the ashen color of the weather, something flashed past. Kelechi would have dismissed it as lightning, except that she could almost swear that she heard a whistle with it.

She had probably eaten too much orange, or her fever had taken more toll that she thought.

Still, in half blind hope, and for lack of destination anyway, she headed in that direction.

As she walked, it became increasingly challenging to put one foot before the other. Her limbs grew heavy and her lids struggled to remain up. When she approached losing consciousness, she bit her lips hard.

Then she saw it. Paved road.

Dizziness a thing of the past now, she dragged her feet towards it, trying to convey the urgency of things to them.

It took her an eternity in her opinion, to finally make it to the shoulder of the road, just in time to see headlights.

She thumbed it, sending a silent prayer to whichever deity had rescued her. But her thumbing turned urgent and eventually to waving as the car got closer with slowing, and eventually zoomed past.

It was the highway, the rain was pelting down hard, and she looked like something a bear vomited, so it was understandable why the car refused to stop for her.

Then the second car, third, eleventh, until she couldn't count again.

Another bout of panic hit her. 'What if no one stopped for her? What if the kidnappers get to her first?'

Cloth and oranges fell as her hands shook too much to hold on to them. Her head hurt more than ever before, and all the living things around her spun till they blended into one swirly entity and blurred where they joined.

Kelechi didn't see the truck moving forward. She didn't realize she was stumbling onto the highway. She didn't even notice that she was moving until she fell, a few seconds from the vehicle

TWELVE

KELECHI FELT HERSELF being tossed like a cloth in the Nile. Later, when she woke, she would remember this moment when she tried to speak, to talk to the trailer driver who had screeched to a stop bare seconds to running her over and loaded her into his truck. She would remember her struggles trying to will his face to appear in single, as opposed to the triple image her eyes showed her. Above all, Kelechi would remember struggling to feel — fear of the unknown person or gratitude at the rescue.

But she couldn't. She had discovered that she was better off in the camp where her fate, like that of others like her, was predictable because it had been sealed.

Now as she stared at the white ceiling, and the IV hanging on a rail with the wire attached to her with a needle, she filled in the gaps for herself. The driver had stopped before running her over and brought her to the hospital.

Kelechi wasn't unaware of what the new development brought. It meant she was out of the bush, of the hood of the kidnappers. She could finally report them. They'd pay for all she'd been through.

But those thoughts passed her by without one sticking long enough to form a plan. She was tired from it all. She wanted to sleep and eat and drink and shower in peace. Still, the thought of shower didn't bring with it any real desire to act it out.

The door opened; she didn't turn to look, and only knew that it opened because of the creaking sound it made.

Kelechi kept her eyes trained on the nurse- at least she supposed the lady standing by her was one, but nothing validated her supposition except that the lady lifted the IV, probably weighing to see what's left.

She let out a long stream of incoherent words. Kelechi knew that she was talking to her in their local dialect, but she didn't understand it, and was sapped of all the energy necessary to nod or shake her head.

The nurse paused, apparently waiting for her response. When none came, she launched again from where she stopped, this time gesticulating.

From her arm movements, Kelechi could tell that she was asking where she lived or a phone number to call, but she didn't respond in any way, didn't even give any hint that she'd heard.

The nurse folded her arms under her breasts and eyed Kelechi, nose turned up, then turned and stalked off.

She left the door open, admitting all kinds of meaningless chatter to Kelechi. As much as she wished the nurse had bothered closing the door, she was relieved that she was alone again. She didn't want anyone talking to or looking at her. She felt unimportant and invisible in a large bulbous world. And the fact that she was not part of it was frightening.

Just when she was beginning to settle down and turn the chatter outside to background noise, the nurse returned. She knew it was her thanks to the slapping sound her slippers made against the cement floor. Did people drag their feet when walking?

But she wasn't alone, another set of footsteps followed hers. Like the first time, she didn't turn to see. They'd come into view eventually.

"Hello, my name is Doctor Goodluck. What is your name?"

Finally, someone who spoke real English. Later she'd ponder on how the lady was a nurse yet didn't speak English. As far as she knew, no school focused exclusively on traditional language.

She kept looking at the doctor. He was dressed in a dirty brown agbada- a reflection of the hospital with its peeling walls. She would have worried whether they injected her with a new needle or if they knew what they were doing, except she didn't care.

"You were brought in yesterday by a man who claimed you ran onto the highway. We couldn't hold him any longer, so he left some hours ago when you didn't wake yesterday."

That was the height of incompetence, but she still didn't mind or say her mind.

"Are you hurting?" Doctor Goodluck asked.

The nurse let out a string of words, though Kelechi couldn't understand a word, she wasn't ignorant of the impatience and annoyance in her voice.

The doctor calmed her down by tapping her shoulder. Still, she made her stance known by tapping the floor with her foot.

"You got an infection from a snake bite. We believe that you were attended to, using local herbs, which would have worked well except that it was administered late. You are malnourished with bruises all over your body. Nothing major, but you need to stay a few more days so we can treat your malaria and pneumonia."

"Thank you," she finally said, as he turned to leave. At least she could say that much, then later she would decide if she should be thankful that she was alive, because at the moment, she was feeling less than alive.

"So, you sabi talk ehn?" the nurse gave the doctor a dark look, then turned back to Kelechi. "Where you from come?"

"Salome let's give her some…"

"We no give her time when we give her medication, na now when it's time to pay she go take time."

"We can just ask her tomorrow."

"You know that I know these people. She knows wetin she dey do. She no want pay. Look her na, she look like person wey get money?"

It occurred to Kelechi that she did indeed look horrible. Her weave had new growths, and without oiling and brushing, she could only imagine how rough the turfs would appear.

Her dressing was another demon altogether. The navy-blue pants which had been well ironed the day she wore it, was now black.

When she said, 'thank you', she noted her breath reeked. She hadn't had the inclination to do anything about it. Still, the knowledge her breath stank like dead fish was unsettling in a way that brought a chill to her skin. "Please, can I have a toothbrush and toothpaste?"

Her question silenced the nurse for a few moments. She looked around as if not quite believing that the patient she was talking down on had spoken. It amused Kelechi. Especially the fact that she didn't know what exactly stunned the nurse. The fact that she had the audacity to make a request which cost money, or she hadn't even been offended or concerned about all she had been saying.

"You want toothbrush and toothpaste?" she asked, taking a couple of steps closer to the bed.

"Yes please," Kelechi said. At some level, she wished that the nurse would pounce on her. Maybe that was what she needed to bring her out of her emotionless daze.

"Sally please, here's some money, get her the brush and paste," the doctor said.

As the nurse stormed out, the doctor fumbled with the drip, then turned to leave. It occurred to Kelechi that she could tell someone about the kidnappers, then when she left, she'd be able to face her life and leave all the ugly memories behind. That way too, she'd fulfill both Ekanem's and Papa's plea of her. She'd then inform the authorities, at least through the doctor, and she won't go back to that nightmare.

"Doctor, I want to tell you what happened to me."

"There's no hurry. Rest, you can tell us when you're better."

"No." The sense of urgency filled her as if she just had to get it over it, now or never. "I really need to say this now."

She wasn't sure at which point in her story the doctor sat beside her, on the tiny low, squeaky hospital bed. Or when he held her hands. Or even when the tears that freely ran down his cheeks began. But she was indifferent to it all. Recounting the tale as if a Nollywood drama she had watched.

Even as she painted the picture of death and bruteness, the story began to look like a lie to her.

She began shaking again. "I'll get a policeman to take your statement, but that will be tomorrow. Now you need to rest, you have exhausted yourself."

She probably had projected her doubt of her own story to the doctor, because in his eyes were expression she couldn't quite read. Maybe he was thinking that she'd lost her sanity. Maybe she had. It would explain a lot of things.

The hair on her neck stood, someone was watching her. She turned towards the door and met the nurse's eyes. She may not have read the doctor's expression, but she read the nurse's quite clearly. On her face were bold, as if written in letters, horror, and fear.

The items she had gotten clattered from her shaky hand to the floor. Even her lips trembled. Then she turned and left.

The rest of the day passed by in a blur, no one came to disturb her except for a little girl who brought her food. Kelechi just slept and woke and repeated the process.

In the darkness, after she'd made peace with the fact that she couldn't hold it in much longer, she made her way outside. It wasn't difficult to navigate because the hospital only had two doors leading out. She took the one closest to her and stepped into the muted darkness.

The fear of having no roof over her head, her first real emotion in a long while, came in fast and strong, propelling her to squat near a bush to ease herself. No electric light shone anywhere, no headlights, and no human sound. She cleaned herself with the cotton wool she'd torn from her medication tray, but not knowing where to dispose of it, she stashed it in her pocket and returned to her room.

But she couldn't sleep, or even think, so she listened to the quiet noise of the night. From the occasional call of an animal in the distance to the whine of mosquitoes at her ears.

Then she heard the footfalls. It wasn't startling, and she had no reason to be afraid, but the sound of them chilled her to her bones. Like the owners were making efforts to keep them from making sounds.

Still, she was unafraid, or at least she wanted to be. She was finally in a place where a scream would attract people, where she was among free people, and where, most importantly, she could navigate to find her house in the state capitol, when she wanted. Still she felt herself stealthily climb down from the bed, and crawl under the cramped under bed and held her breath.

Her experience had turned her into a paranoid crazy woman.

She was about to release her breath when the door was kicked open and a flood of light from different torches filled the room with brightness.

"Where is she?"

Her heart didn't beat wildly, at least she'd credit herself for that, but it did much worse. It stopped. Sweat beaded her forehead and trickled down her face, neck, and back. Her palms were clammy, yet she shivered with cold.

The voice was one she would never forget as long as she lived. Mr. Kimaiyo.

"She been lie here o!" the nurse's voice came.

"And as she's not here, where is she?"

"I tell you say she lie here this night when I go call you people."

"You say she spoke of us?"

"Nawa o oga, why are you sounding like this? You think I will suffer to go inside there to call you if I am not sure of what I heard with my koro ears?"

"You should have taken better care of her. You know how serious this is?"

"Abeg it's not me who lost her in the first place. Abi I shouldn't have gone to call you?"

"You did well," Mr. Kimaiyo intervened, in a too cool voice, and Kelechi imagined him pulling a trigger on the nurse's head. But his voice continued, instead of a gunshot. "Who is this doctor she told the story to?"

"That one is an otondo. He doesn't know anything. In fact, he did not believe her sef."

"Take me to his house."

"You go kill am?" she asked in a voice one would use to ask if you wanted to buy carrots. Kelechi loathed her more than anything she'd ever hated.

"No, at least not if I determine that he thinks what you say he does and has no hand in the whereabouts of the girl."

"Oya na, let us go, me, I want to go to sleep, I am tired."

"You and you, stay here, you, come with us, three of you go round the village, keep your ears and eyes open. Check the police station too and every hotel."

Kelechi waited until all settled. She couldn't keep her position; the room was empty save for herself. She crawled out and tiptoed to the door. It was open, which was good, because she saw the two men at each doorway. She was trapped.

THIRTEEN

THERE WAS NO way to leave the hospital, yet staying wasn't an option either. Not only could either of the men come into the room at any moment, but as dawn drew nearer, others would return, discounting the hospital staffs themselves.

Kelechi clenched her fists, willing her emotions under control so she could at least think coherent thoughts.

Then it came to her, in the form of the moon shining, like the universe was on her side. The window.

The small opening was raised high in a way that discredits the builders, but she couldn't afford to spend time critiquing the work of the architects.

She tried shoving the bed closer to the wall, but the metal feet holding up clanked against the floor. Any more noise and she'd have company.

Then worse, the cock crowed. Kelechi had to act and act fast.

She crept close to the wall and stood propped against the boulder. One of the men was smoking, and the other, on his phone. They were both alert. She had expected them to be sleepy or just lax.

There was a low stool in the corridor farther up near where the phone operator stood. There was no way she could reach it without either of them noticing.

There really wasn't any choice. She could wait out her fate, make a run for it from either door or try to get the chair. She decided to put her money- or as it was, her life- in the latter. There was no doubt about the men being fully armed, and even less doubt on their readiness to use it.

She removed her slippers and hid under the bed. Whatever happened, she didn't want anything that'd implicate or endanger Papa. She watched the movements of the men closely. The smoker was a fidgeter. He turned this way and that with each draw on his weed. But in the long minutes that she observed them, he didn't turn back. He didn't expect his prey would be behind. The phone man stood bent over, immersed by what he was doing. Unlike Smoker, he neither turned left nor right or even back. His mobile phone commanded his full attention.

The challenge was stepping into the corridor, where both men could see her if they simply turned a little. Then move straight up until the block of rooms to her right shielded her from Smoker. Finally, she'd have just Phone Man to be mindful of, who she had to get about fifty meters closer to get to the chair.

Kelechi said a short prayer with her eyes open and fixed on the chair. Her request was simple: Lord, I won't die at the hands of these two men. Maybe it was not really a request.

She stepped into the corridor, walking with just her toes, holding her breath. And careful not to make any sudden movements that'll attract reflexive vision, she made her way to the door of the room, free from chances of being spotted by Smoker, but still at risk with Phone Man.

Staying close to the wall was risking being in the peripheral sightline of the kidnapper ahead of her, so she walked instead, in the middle of the corridor, still on her toes rather than on her whole feet.

She made it to the chair uneventfully, and as she lifted it as carefully as she could, eyes fixated on the man ahead of her, she could see from the display on his screen, that he wasn't really holding a phone, but a Gameboy. It was the same man with whom Ekanem had come to serve them food.

The memories of Ekanem brought sadness in such a wave that she clutched the chair to her chest to keep from acting out.

But it was a wrong move. The wood hit the metal of her necklace, making a tiny noise, but noise audible in the stillness of approaching dawn.

Kelechi froze, waiting for the man to turn his head, and prepared to hit him with the chair if he did.

But he didn't. He was so ensconced in his gaming that he hadn't registered or minded the sound. Kelechi considered hitting him anyway, at least that would mean that the kidnappers would be one man shorter. But the risks far outweighed the victory. She might aim and miss, or her blow may not be hard enough, or struggle between them might ensure drawing the attention of the smoking killer- all of which meant death for her.

Instead, she retraced her footsteps, too afraid to turn, but walking backward, though expecting to bump into a hard chest at any moment.

She didn't, she only turned when the door of the room to her right came into view. Then she turned, being mindful of the smoker now. But he too didn't turn as she reentered her room. All of that may have happened in just a couple of minutes because she only let out her breath as she stepped into the room that had now become a temporary haven.

She had been afraid, though refusing to think of her fears, of the chair not being high enough to get her to the window. She needn't have bothered. The wall was already low as it was, and with the additional height granted by the stool, she easily reached the window. However, another problem posed. The opening was too narrow to fit her frame.

The plank acting as a door to the opening was decayed, needing just a good pressure to set it free, but her hands numbed by fear couldn't quite give that. She needed something to pry the hinge off. Afraid to come down, she surveyed the room for anything that might be useful, but the room was bare.

She removed her necklace and using the sharp end, dug inside the rotten wood, near the bottom hinge. In no time, she got to the metal, and with nothing for support, the wood gave way, dangling from the top hinge still attached.

She could stay and try to get it totally free, but with this little victory, she was too eager to wait a minute longer. The chair wasn't high enough for her to swing her leg over, so nudging the wood aside, and poking her head out, then her shoulders, till her feet left the stool. But hanging with her waist down in and stomach up out, she had nothing to hold on to for support. She became trapped with the upper half of her out and the lower half of her in. All she could do was let herself fall. She examined the ground beneath, just a few meters of dirt and then grass which started low and grew steadily tall. Falling wouldn't do her much harm, so she fell, landing with a thud. Gripped by fear that she may have been heard, she dashed straight into the bush. But that brought with it the uncomfortable memory of her days in the jungle, so she dashed out again, onto a narrow pathway, but close enough to the bush so she could dive in at the sight of anyone approaching.

*****

The appearance of the sun, or even its fading did not do anything to Kelechi, except mark another day of survival. From the hospital, it had just been a day of more trekking.

The village had nothing in it except for ancient people and few children, with even fewer youths. They made their revenue from farming and trading the produce.

The sun, though less harsh than in the forest, was still scorching, and without any tree shade, she was worse off than in the forest. The only good thing was that here, she could see people.

Apart from the pap and dry bread that a little girl brought in for her in the hospital almost twenty-four hours ago, she hadn't had any other thing to eat. At least in the forest she had fruits. Kelechi began to wonder whether she made progress at all, or consistently jumping from the frying pan to fire.

She almost knocked on doors to beg for water, but the fear that no one could be trusted prevented her. If she could not trust a medical worker, then random humans were an even bigger risk to take. With the resilience she'd been forced to learn since her kidnap, she kept telling herself *'one more hour then I'll ask the next person I come across'*. Still, after each hour, she'd extend it.

Now, night was fast approaching, and she was hungry, bushed, sleepy, and tired of her aimless and endless journey.

She traveled through town, careful to keep to crowds when in an open place and stick near the bush when in a lonely place.

She stole a pair of bathroom slippers from a compound whose occupants were out. She also considered swiping a dress to change the stinky one she wore but reasoned that that would be spotted too easily by the owner. In the house from which she borrowed the slippers, she also lifted a couple of N200 notes. It wasn't enough for transportation, but with it at least, she could call her office. All that was needed was a payphone, which she discovered was a difficult thing in a town as tiny as this.

As Kelechi passed by a tuck-shop, her stomach grumbled with the thought of biting into the golden-brown donut displayed in the stained show glass.

'You only live once,' she muttered to herself as if she needed to justify walking up to the owner and asking for the dough. She repeated the mantra before asking for a bottle of soft drink. She may be caught at any moment, so she should at least eat to gather strength to face whatever comes. Besides, if she lived till tomorrow, she could always loot another home.

"Please can I have a corkscrew?" she asked the seller. The young lady let out a spree of words in the local dialect which Kelechi didn't understand. "Opener," she repeated.

"I said we don't have, Use your teeth na." The lady was nice, she didn't look offended at all, but her friend with whom she was gisting with looked irritated as if it was common to uncork a bottle with your teeth and Kelechi was just being nasty by interrupting their conversation.

"I can't possibly-"she remembered she needed to blend in, but her face fell at the thought of what she was expected to do. Her classmates used to it a lot, but even as a teen, Kelechi refused, and now the situation attempted to make her break her principle.

Kelechi opened her mouth to ask the lady to return it and refund her but shut it when the lady beat her to it. "Bring it, I will open it for you."

"With your teeth?" Kelechi felt a puke rise in her throat at the thought of it.

"Yes," the lady answered, smiling.

"No, thanks. I will open it myself." The other lady rolled her eyes. Not that the seller had a bad breath, in fact, her teeth were pearly white and well set, which may explain why she was so quick to laugh, and it would be cleaner than Kelechi's unwashed own. But she'd rather use hers than drink from a bottle whose cork had been removed by another person's mouth.

She hadn't brushed in weeks, hadn't had a proper bath, hadn't changed her clothes, or taken care of her hair. Even her pubic hair was crying for attention, now she had to open her bottle cork using her teeth. How much lower would she go before the universe smiled at her?

She took her pendant again, to see if there's a way she could pry the cork off without having to use her teeth. In reflex, she pressed the button to ensure that was off to avoid damaging the camera.

Then cold sweat began to bead her forehead. She wore her necklace all through, and the camera had been on. Since the day she received it, it became a habit of hers to put it on every morning after dressing for work, and off at night. She vividly recalled putting it on in the morning of her kidnap and knew very well that she hadn't put it off if anything, she had forgotten about it or what it meant.

Her pendant had a 5 GB memory space which when on, stored video and audio recordings!

FOURTEEN

THE KNOWLEDGE THAT something positive was happening fueled Kelechi. She found that uncorking the bottle using her teeth wasn't as bad or difficult as she imagined. She ate her doughnuts, each bite tastier than the last, and washed it down with her drink.

Eager to leave and start planning, she forgot to collect her balance and had to be called back for it. At first, when she was called, she stiffened, afraid that the ladies were accomplices and had found out about the recorder.

As she walked down the road, head swimming with plans and possibilities, she removed the necklace and clutched the pendant in her palm, while winding the chain around her wrist.

Darkness was descending and market women were returning to the village. Chatters in an unknown language filled everywhere with life and sounds of pestle meeting mortar as women prepared dinner brought with it, the aroma of traditional food, which until then, she hadn't really allowed herself to miss.

Then she saw them. It was difficult not to, with their gait and all. Even villagers took notice of their difference and made way for them when they passed.

Kelechi had almost given in to her urge to sprint for her life when it occurred to her that they hadn't seen her. Well not that they hadn't seen her, but they hadn't picked her apart. With her stolen worn slippers, brown and dirty pants, blouse which was hanging on her because she had lost so much weight, and her unkempt hair. Also, the kidnappers didn't really know who they were looking for. All they knew was that she is young and running from them. They probably came out the way they did to make her react the way she almost had. They expected her to run when she noticed them.

As they approached, she grew shakier. They might not know her, but that didn't stop any of them from recognizing her when they get close enough.

Her breakthrough came in the form of a narrow way that snaked off from the road. She noticed it almost the same time she reached it. With her only other choice being to keep moving ahead, she dashed in without pausing to think. As she walked, swiftly increasing her pace, her thoughts were not on where or what the path led to, but on the possibility that she might be heading exactly where they were going. Conscious of never turning to avoid showing her nervousness and fear, already aware that her sudden turn into the track road may have alerted them, she kept moving without turning.

They didn't follow her into the narrow path. She knew this only when she entered a sudden left bend on the pathway. She used that opportunity to look back the way she had come.

There was no sign of them anywhere, just a couple of women entering the path she had taken and chatted. In substitute for punching the air in victory, Kelechi clenched her jaw and fists, the pressure pressing the silver pendant in her palm.

The path narrowed and twisted until it widened then opened in into a clearing. She passed a stinking little zinc house, which she assumed was a public toilet. A well-kept little square house stood a few feet from a large building. She categorized it as big based on the houses and huts she'd observed in the village. Even before she saw the pattern stained windows, she recognized a church.

Even though she had been falling off her Faith, the church brought her a sense of hope, comfort, and peace. Somehow, she knew that once in the house of God, it'd then really be God's duty to take care of her. She wouldn't need to work so hard for herself, God will handle it all.

Humbled by what she felt, which she hadn't experienced from the moment she raised her eyes from her tablet in the taxi, she stood at the huge door- which wouldn't have felt huge a few weeks ago- taking the 'welcome' written there very personally, as if the Angels with their wings spread apart, where talking to her – knew her, and didn't mind her state of raggedness. She felt tears welling up in her eyes, and without the need to hold them or wipe them, they fell freely down her cheeks.

The doors opened, revealing a small man. He was smiling at her through his thick reading glasses. "Welcome child," he said.

He wasn't dressed like a priest, but she knew that catholic Fathers addressed their parishioners as he just did. It could be from his paternal look or the overwhelming sense of safety she felt, but she felt her chest growing hard, and her lips trembling. The women she had seen had arrived and were calling a cheerful greeting to the Father who expertly answered them by names, asking after things and people while also cooing her. Other women were also entering from another route, a place she would come to know as the main entrance.

"Come here child." Father led her by the shoulders into the haven, through pews until he got to the middle, and led on until the middle of the rows. "Sit here, I will come to you after mass."

In a little while, the church grew in the number of attendees, but no one seemed interested in her section of the pew. She was almost invisible.

A man entered and exchanged greetings with some of the members of the congregation, then went to the platform and began services. Used to having every member a local, he spoke mainly in the local dialect, launching into English only on occasion.

When he finished, he stepped down, leaving the stage for Father, who had changed into his white robe.

The priest brought with him a message of hope and peace. A sermon that brought nostalgia to Kelechi with force. He reminded her of Pastor Emeka from children's church, who made the world look easy, and paradise seem like a place one cannot afford to miss. As she grew, she found herself thinking of what Pastor Emeka would do in whichever situation she faced. In her years in university, she had searched for a church that taught the same values as Pastor Emeka: Keep all the ten commandments of God and you'll be rewarded both in heaven and on earth. She discovered he was right, if she told the truth, she was never punished. She had even fantasized about marrying Pastor Emeka, and it devastated her when he got married, and the blow hurt more when he married an ugly girl who didn't attend their church.

In the middle seat on the middle pew in the church, she listened closely, hungry for the dish Father served, and rapt so as not to miss a single morsel.

She was sad when he concluded service. She yearned for more. It was as if he was speaking directly to her soul. Father greeted his parishioners, smiling and patient, saying the rosary with one, then the sign of the cross with another. He seemed tireless, weaving through old men and women, and a few youths, with the children running around.

The worshippers all dispersed before he approached her. "How are you, my daughter? You seem calmer."

"Thank you, Father." She felt her lips widen in an effortless laugh.

"Do you have a place to stay for the night?"

It hit Kelechi that she had been so contented that she had forgotten all about the danger that she faced, even to the point of not worrying about the basic things that she should worry about- like food, bath, sleep, and a phone. "No."

"I have a free room. You should stay here tonight."

"Thank you," she said, humbled.

Father remained quiet as they strolled towards the building at the side. At the house, he unlocked a door, opening straight to what she couldn't decide if it was the living room or waiting room, or counseling room, or all. It was sparsely furnished, with four plastic chairs, a plastic table in the center, a low wooden table covered with a white cloth, on which sat a gigantic Bible, a huge chaplet, cross, and effigies and whatnot, all religious stuff. It should have made Kelechi uncomfortable as she'd never been a catholic, but she found that they didn't offend her at all.

"Your room is the second door," Father said pointing to his right. The last is a bathroom, you can freshen up first. There's a new bar of soap, and toothbrush, but the towels aren't new, and I don't have a sponge, I'm afraid."

"Thank you, Father, really."

"Thank God."

She had missed this too, she found. In the world she'd put herself, people said 'you're welcome' or 'anytime' when thanked. Her mother always responded with a 'Thank God', and so had Pastor Emeka.

It felt good to rub soap down her body. The soap wasn't like she was used to. She found a Lux and plenty black soaps. She chose a wrap of black soap, not because she preferred it, in truth, at home she used a very expensive soap, and she'd rather use Lux which had a label, not to mention that they'd advertised with her company before, than a local soap which no care had been taken in the production, not to mention the absence of a NAFDAC registration number, but she took it anyway.

The soap smelled musky, and to her approval, bubbled generously. Without sponge, but with a tall drum of clean water, she rubbed her skin hard with her bare hand, then washed the suds off with water and repeated the process. The longer she bathed, the better she felt, until a rap sounded on the door. She knew she was alone in the whole house with a man, yet she wasn't the least bit afraid. Instead, she felt safe.

"I'm almost done," she said, washing off the latest bubbles.

"Oh, take your time. I brought a shirt for you. I don't have any female clothing, but these would cover you up."

"Thank you, sir."

"You are blessed. I also found a towel. It's old, but it's clean. You'll find both outside the door."

"OK, Sir." She listened to the rhythm of his retreating footfalls. He had a way he walked — systematic, a limp in his right leg. She dumped her dirty clothes in an empty iron bucket, then on second thought, she added water and poured the whole content of a mini-sized sachet of detergent in it. She shouldn't expect Father or anyone who did his laundry to do hers too.

Just like when she was having her bath, she kept pouring out the dirty soapy water and restarting the washing. She would have continued, except for the continuous growling of her stomach in response to the aroma of proper food. She had been assaulted by those since before she found the church. Too bad she couldn't knock on a random door and beg for food.

The shirt Father hung out for her on a nail protruding from the bathroom door was at least six times larger than her. It went over her knees and the sleeves covered the length of her arms even though she had folded them repeatedly. There was a short too, which was unnecessary. But considering that she was in the house of a Reverend Father and alone with him, no less, she put them on. That too was too large and too long. But at least, the waist held, and it felt good to be in clean clothes again, never mind that they were not hers, still, the freeness of them appeared to be exactly what she needed. A chance for her body to breathe.

In the multipurpose room, Kelechi's eyes lit up at the sight that greeted her. There was Father, in a blue striped apron, serving hot rice and stew.

She took extra-long strides and was beside him in mere moments. She would beg if only she could have a spoonful. Her body shook, and fresh sweat beaded her forehead. She knew she was starving, but she had never understood the overreaction of starved children at the sight of food, until now.

"Join me." Father positioned two chairs before the centered table, and sat on one, motioning her to the other.

Kelechi forgot all mannerisms and etiquette. She didn't wait for the invitation to be repeated, and even as Father broke out in a rhythmic prayer of thanks, she was already digging in, hands shaking as she lifted the spoon to her mouth. She didn't have the luxury of chewing, swallowing the grains which thankfully, were cooked soft.

Father didn't seem to mind that she started off. He concluded his prayers and took his spoon, but instead of eating, he watched Kelechi, a paternal smile on his face. He didn't disturb her or try to engage her in a conversation as she ate.

"Would you like some more?" he asked when she finished. She nodded and accepted his bowl. "You should drink some water to aid digestion."

She nodded again and accepted the cup he offered her. After downing the content, she resumed eating, this time more slowly.

"What is your name?" Father asked.

"Kelechi. Thank you so much for the food, Sir."

"Thank God. Will that be enough for you?"

"Yes, thanks." For the first time, she noted that he wasn't eating. "Where's your own food?" Father looked at his plate, set before Kelechi and winked at her. Her cheeks burned in embarrassment. "I am so sorry."

"You shouldn't be. I gave it up myself."

"But what will you eat?"

"Man shall not live by bread alone. Don't worry about me, child, our heavenly father who takes care of the birds of the air will not allow me to die just for missing a meal. Besides, if I do die, it will be a gain."

Kelechi was about to ask how that was, but Father was smiling, so she did too. She cleared the table and insisted on doing the dishes, and by the time she finished, she was so exhausted that she struggled to be on her feet.

Father was reading the Bible when Kelechi made her way to the room, he gave her. She couldn't stay awake long enough to note anything about the room, except that the bed was bigger than that of the hospital. And when she crashed on it, she found herself in heaven

FIFTEEN

THE SUN GLEAMED through the gaps in the window at Kelechi, which was the reason why she woke up, otherwise, she may have slept through the whole day.

There were two notes stuck on the door:

Good morning, Kelechi, I am leaving for Mass. There is tea and bread in the kitchen, you can help yourself.

The other read:

I am back from Mass, but I am going for visitation. I expect to return before the evening mass. There's food in the warmer on the table. God bless you.

At the thought of food, Kelechi's stomach rumbled. She wondered if she'd be a food freak for life. She ate the garri and soup the Reverend had left her, did the dishes, and had her bath, this time taking a little less than she had the previous night.

She finished putting on her own clothes, now dry, when she remembered the necklace. But it wasn't in the bathroom, the multipurpose room, or her room.

In the necklace was the evidence she would need to bring the gang down and save many lives — if she decides to, which wasn't in her plans yet. Still, knowing it's there gave her what she didn't want to think of as hope. She couldn't possibly have lost something so important.

She combed the house; living room, her room, the bathroom, and the kitchen, but she couldn't find her gold necklace, and most importantly, the pendant.

The day was waning, the sun moving steadily west. The clock read 5:11. The evening service would begin at six, and the Reverend Father would return before then. She ran out of the house, not a bit conscious of the wrong people seeing her and headed for the church building. Part afraid that it would be locked, but thankfully, the door swung in when she pushed.

Kelechi started at the center of the middle pew where she had sat during the sermon, half expecting to see the gleam of the chain, and half knowing that she would not. She went through all the pews in the center, crouching under each and combing the length. She went slowly, careful not to miss a spot. She still went the length of the church, center pew, left and right pews. She even extended her search to the altar, wishing that the statues adorning the place would be merciful and make the chain appear even if it weren't there. They showed mercy all right, but only in their pitied looks. She ran back out, retracing her footsteps a day ago, going all the way to the main road, from where she had entered the track to avoid the kidnappers.

Returning to the house, Kelechi's resolve was set. If she didn't carelessly lose the necklace, then someone must have taken it, and only one person had come close to her since the last time she saw her necklace. The Reverend Father may be working with the killers too. She berated herself for being so trusting of him because of his religious status. If a nurse was in, then it was illogical to discount a Reverend Father.

She picked a good-sized rock as she was entering the house, and smashed the padlock closing the priest's room.

She started with the cloth hanger, a long wooden and outdated wall hanger. She brought each cloth down, searching their pockets one after the other. She took down everything on the tables, stripped his bed of its sheet, and searched everywhere else. Still, she couldn't find it, then she went to the kitchen for a knife to unlock the chests.

"What is wrong?" The priest returned while she was away and was by the door doing the sign of the cross.

Kelechi had forgotten that he'd be back anytime, and she was disoriented, she hadn't thought of what she'd say or do when he arrived.

"Kelechi, what happened here?"

"Are they coming, or will you kill me yourself?"

The priest made the sign of the cross. "Nobody will kill anybody."

"I know you are working with the kidnappers, no need to keep pretending. I was too stupid to think you, a priest, won't be involved, even after the hospital."

"Which kidnappers?" He did another sign of the cross and kissed the statue dangling from it. "What hospital?"

"Have you given them my necklace? You might destroy the evidence, but trust me, if not me, another person will put an end to you butchers!"

"This?" he held up a thin chain, Kelechi's necklace.

"I knew it was you!"

"I found this on the ground behind the stairs this morning. It was the same place we met, so I kept it to ask you before I ask the rest of the congregation."

"Oh my God!" Kelechi slumped down, tears flowing down her cheeks like water from the Nile. It felt good to be wrong because not only did she have her necklace back, but she was safe too. "You really aren't working with the killers?"

"God save my soul, no, never! This is the first time I am hearing about such. Tell me about them."

By the time she finished her story, the priest was sitting beside her on the floor, engulfing her in an embrace. When he pulled away, she realized how much he had shielded her. She felt cold and exposed.

"So, your necklace recorded everything?"

"Yes," she whispered.

"I hope it didn't run out of space."

"It wouldn't. It has five GB space, and even while it is turned on, it goes to sleep after a few minutes of no sensed motion."

"That's great, now we can get them, even if it means calling foreign help."

"How can we do that?"

"Well first, we need to check the evidence and know exactly what we have."

"I'm so sorry for tearing your house apart," she said when the priest had difficulty finding his laptop."

"It's understandable. No one should go through what you did. Praise God for the strength he has given you to endure."

Kelechi wasn't sure if she had had strength, and if so, if it was from God. But he sounded so convinced, so she left it at that.

The video was real and in 3D. It didn't capture what she didn't see, because it faced front, so everything she saw was recorded.

The priest kept mumbling prayers with his rosary. She couldn't make herself look at his laptop screen. She had lived through the nightmare once, and she wasn't going to live it again, especially if she would be the one to subject herself to that. The Reverend's face changed expressions from sadness to anger, to pain, horror, and a host of many others that Kelechi couldn't keep track of.

In the end, he gave up when the fighting madam and house girl were separated and one shot. He wouldn't go longer even though Kelechi assured him that more was ahead. He only scrolled to the end to check if it took in everything. And it did.

"This is pure horror, and to think that a human, created in the image and likeness of God, by God himself is capable of doing this, I can never understand how they allowed the devil to use them to such extent."

Kelechi didn't think it was fair to heap the blame on the devil, but she kept her peace.

"Please, may I use your phone? I need to check in with my family to assure them that I am alright and to also call my staff. I'll need a lot of things."

Kelechi got the phone and managed to live through her mother's hysteria. Then she called her secretary, Alice. It was late and she figured no one would be at the office. She was right, Alice was at home, and after the fuss, she got her to take down a list of the things she'd need.

As she slept, Kelechi felt everything click back to its place. Alice would arrange for an escorted car, speak with the military, and get things started with the media. She would also wire some money to her so that she could at least shop for some clothes and look a bit presentable.

It felt good to have things going again, to be able to predict what would happen next, and most of all, to be in charge once more.

If all went well, her media company will keep the headlines for weeks, especially as she would get exclusives during the investigations and arrests. She'd make sure of that.

She woke up early, as Father prepared for the morning mass. It was the day her new story was to begin, and she didn't want to miss any part of it.

Father had let her keep his phone through the night and morning as she called everyone who would be useful. The ball was rolling and on her terms.

When Father came in, almost limp running, before the time he had said he would, she knew that something was wrong. She had felt it all day in the way her heart would suddenly skip, her skin breaks out in sweats, and her body shaking. Under all the hopeful planning, she had known on a deeper level, though refused to admit it that it was all too good to be true. It wouldn't work because it was all a sham. This was not a fairy tale that had happy endings. Here was a reality, and, the bad guys always won.

"Kelechi, you need to run for your life!" Father said even before he entered the door. "I saw them, some of the men from your video and even new ones with them. I don't know how they found out about you."

"Where are they?"

"Waiting for me. They came with some military men, told my catechist that they are the escort you as requested by your secretary."

"How would they know about my call to Alice?"

"Did you give your details in the hospital?"

"Shit! Sorry. They needed it in order to bill my card."

"I told them to wait while I finish with my visitor. I slipped out through the alter door. I can't keep them waiting for long."

"Thank you, sir." Kelechi unplugged her USB and fastened it back to her necklace, making sure to clamp it before she went.

"Kelechi, here." He handed her a key. "My car is parked just inside the gate. From here they won't see you, but from the car, you will be in sight. Be careful. I don't have a full tank, and I don't have money either, but here's all the money I have on me, I hope it'll be enough to set you off until you can figure out what to do next."

"Thank you, sir."

"Also, wear this." he thrust a bundle of white and blue fabric into her arms. "It's a habit and it should disguise you."

Short of words, she hugged him tight, and took off.

As Kelechi begged the old Nissan to kick up, she felt eyes on her. Finally, the car started, and she drove off, but on the other side of the gate was Mr. Kimaiyo.

SIXTEEN

KELECHI FROZE, HER palm sweaty against the leather of the steering. Mr. Kimaiyo stepped directly onto her path. She considered running back, but all he had to do was shoot her. With his khaki, he didn't need to justify the public killing, at worse he could just label her a criminal and no one would question him.

She could also run him over, that is if the metal the priest used for mobility was strong enough to kill someone. But if she did, she would officially become a criminal, and worse, she'd be a killer for life.

Her only option was to face her nightmare. The last time she saw them, they hadn't recognized her, but if they knew of the call she put to her office, they must also have seen her picture.

"Please, can you move,t sir?" She gave him a smile which she hoped got to her eyes. She prayed that the habit she was wearing would offer a good enough disguise.

He looked past her car, and then gave her a small nod and too friendly laugh. "Bless you, Sister."

From the rear-view, she saw the Reverend lead other camouflaged men towards his house. She didn't know what he planned and hoped it worked. But he was God's property. She left Him to handle him.

It was pure freedom to be behind wheels, at her pace, and heading to a destination she knew. Without a passport or license, she found that the habit was of great help at checkpoints. Policemen didn't stop her but made way for her and offered greetings. The downside was that she had to smile and be friendly to everybody who waved or cheered.

The car lurched every now and then, but it kept driving distance between her and what she was running from.

In the late afternoon, the engine died. She tried everything she knew to get it back on the road, but it wouldn't budge. The fuel gauge wasn't working so she had no way of knowing how much diesel was in it. In the town before, she had stopped for lunch in a roadside eatery beside a gas station, and though she had thought of topping up, she decided against it. Father had given her 5000 Naira and eating alone had cost her 2000 Naira, she didn't know what awaited her on the road and the journey was still far, so she decided to keep the cash for as long as she could.

"Sister, Sister!"

A group of boys approached her and even though she didn't know these parts, she wasn't naïve. She knew it was no big deal to be robbed, raped, and even killed.

"Your car broke?" one of them who didn't look eighteen yet, asked.

"Yes, my dear." She tried to put on her most matronly look, hoping it was good enough from a novice who had never had to play the part before.

"What happened to it?"

This was the type of question that would make her walk away in a normal situation. "I don't know. It just stopped."

"Where are you going?" the older, looking a few years older asked.

"Abuja."

"Ha, that's a very far distance!"

"Yes o, and it's impossible for you to get there today or even tomorrow." The younger joined.

"Especially with your kind of car."

"But sister, how do you plan to go to Abuja in this vehicle? It's a very far distance and that's why your car broke down. It's worn out."

"It's already night. These parts can be very dangerous for a man alone at this time, and even more for a woman."

"Yes o, it's late and even a reverend sister is still a woman."

"What should I do now?" The prospect of entering the hands of another gang was not an appealing one.

"You know what? My brother and I are heading home now, come with us. We will get some boys from the hood to push your car to the village mechanic's shop. He'll repair it and you can continue your journey."

Kelechi seemed unsure. These village boys wouldn't just offer her a bed and help without anything. People didn't do favors for anyone who couldn't pay them, and so far, she hadn't made any offers to them.

"She still dey consider? I don't think she needs help. Musa, let's go abeg." the younger boy said.

"Ahmed, nawa for you oh. This is a reverend sister you're talking about so o. After all, we are strangers, it's normal for her to think it through. You'd do the same in her position."

"Ah sister sorry oh, I didn't mean it like that."

When Kelechi smiled at them, she found that she meant it. It was true that people hardly offered help for free, but looking back at her journey so far, she had received help for free from unlikely places. The world was scary all right, but there was still good in it.

"Thank you very much, Musa and…"

"Ahmed, ma."

"Ahmed, thank you. God will bless you for your offer."

The walk through the narrow pathway made in the bush brought back fear and ugly memories. Kelechi found herself listening for screams, looking for snakes, and dead bodies. At some point, she clutched Musa's arm to assure herself that he was there, and not a figment of her imagination leading her back to her nightmares.

"No fear, Sister we are the owner of this hood. As long as you're with me no maga would date touch you."

Kelechi found herself believing in those words, and they made her hold on tighter.

The village was like the others, rural with more of the aged than the young. It was almost dark, and most people were in their homes. The ones who saw her waved and called. A couple invited her to dinner and even a mother ran after them with a sickly child.

"Pray for my son, Sister!" the woman cried, "Tell Mary to beg God. She had children so she would understand."

It was Musa that came to her rescue. "Sister don tire, mama Priye. Take him go to baba, let him see a doctor."

Kelechi hoped that the woman would take Musa's advice. One look at the child, she could tell that he was suffering from malnutrition. She could stop and advise the crying mother on what vegetables and supplements to give her son, she could even draw a rough meal timetable to ensure that they ate balanced meals with what they had, but that may blow her cover, and even though she didn't know the reach of her pursuers, she couldn't risk it.

Into the night, a scream would wake the village, and in the morning, Kelechi would learn that little Priye had died, and she would shed tears. Her pain would be at the knowledge that she could have done something, knowing it would have been too late. It still did not assuage her self blame. She would be sad because since her kidnap, death had become so real and so close to her. She would feel a personal pain because it would bring back Ifeoma and her baby. Her misery would make her uncomfortable in the village and at down, she would ask to leave.

Her hosts were gracious, too gracious in fact that she was uncomfortable. From the oil-fueled lantern purging dark smoke to the watery soup, she knew that things were tough for them, yet they served her with the biggest chunks of meat and fish, leaving their sons with none. They thought she wouldn't notice, but she did, including that her watery soup was in fact, thicker than that of the rest.

After the meal, the woman offered to accompany her to the bathroom. She was in her fifties and had the potential of looking beautiful with the right clothes, soap, meals, and rest, but by her looks, she may as well be twice that. The bathroom was appalling — a dingy little zinc enclosure, small enough that you couldn't make the slightest of movements with your body brushing their sides. There was a large stone occupying one end, and on it lay a dish containing almost washed out soaps. Part of it was smoother and cleaner, and Kelechi suspected that they cleaned their feet there.

The woman placed the oil lamp just outside the open door of the bathroom. Kelechi wondered if she was expected to have her bath in the roofless and door-less space. She was about to thank her and say that she didn't want a bath when the woman beat her to it.

"It's not much, but it's already night, so you can bathe in the bush. Nothing will happen." She sounded shy.

"It is fine, thank you again for your hospitality," Kelechi found herself saying.

"Ah, this is such a great honor o. For a Reverend Sister to be our guest is not a small matter. It means God is in our house today." She handed Kelechi a bar of new soap.

She passed a stick between the opening of the door and hung her wrapper on it, allowing it to drape to the floor, solving the open-door issue. At least no one would be looking in through the top, unless God of course, and since He sees her all the time anyway, it didn't matter much.

"When you remove your clothes, pass it to me so that it won't fall."

Kelechi did as she was told, handing the habit over, but not her underwear. She hung those on a protruding part of the zinc.

They offered her the hammock to sit as they gathered out to take in the cool night breeze before going to sleep, but she declined. They had been gracious enough, and allowing them to sit on the spread-out mat while she balanced on the hammock was something she couldn't find herself doing. Above all, Kelechi was conscious of the fact that while they may open their home to a stranger, they wouldn't go through these extra miles if the stranger was not a Reverend Sister. She was a fraud and more than once, she found herself very close to telling them so.

The okada man who they had called to drop her off when she had insisted to go early the next morning stopped her at the junction where her hosts had advised. He couldn't go farther because of a feud she hadn't paid close attention to. They had loaded her with instructions on where to go from there.

"Thank you." She swung down. "How much?"

"Ah don't worry, Sister. Market will be good today as I carried a Reverend on my bike!" The bike man smiled ear to ear. She wondered if he left the money for her or her hosts paid him prior.

When Kelechi insisted on continuing her journey that early, without waiting for her car, she hadn't factored the attention of wearing a habit, even in a core northern state like Maiduguri. Everyone seemed too eager to help and when she entered a public bus going to the motor park, those sitting beside her were uncomfortable and excited at the same time. And when she got down, several people offered to pay her fare.

She chose to get down because she didn't want the attention the habit brought to follow her to the park, and eventually to Abuja. The bus stop she had gotten down at with some passengers was in a market. Sellers were just opening their shops, and not many were very interested in her.

Kelechi entered the first shop she saw where clothes were sold. The seller, a young girl of about thirteen was hanging out clothes, probably setting up the shop before the day sales began when her mother or whoever would take over. She assisted Kelechi in picking out the right sized jeans and a t-shirt in ash. She felt bad about bargaining with a child, but that was until the haggling began. The girl may be a child, but she wasn't new at what she did. When Kelechi left with her new purchase, she was feeling ripped, and may not be far from the truth, as the girl kept beaming as she walked away. She made a mental note to self: *When bargaining with a child, be extra hard because they will be, and if you're not careful, their innocent face will mislead you.*

She kept walking about the market until she spotted a bathroom with a sign: *Urinate N20, Shit N50.* But some minutes later, when she came out wearing her new outfit, she saw no one to give the money to. They probably weren't out yet, but she didn't feel guilty walking away. She did not wee or poo.

Feeling good and ready to conquer the world, Kelechi entered another bus going to the Park. She shouldn't have bothered. At the park, the ticket to Abuja was N17,020 but she had just N540 left, and worse, she had dumped the habit at the urinary, if she still had it, getting help wouldn't have been so hard.

Except that dumping it was a blessing in disguise, because Mr. Kimaiyo and his men, not quite trusting the priest's words, were also looking for a Reverend sister in blue and white habits, driving an old Nissan.

Kelechi spent the day walking listlessly, and when night came, she went with the flow of people going to their respective homes. When the night became still and everyone sleeping, she walked up to the doors of a house and slept.

The shove of the door against her ribs woke her. The man of the house was standing at the other side of the door poking out his head at her.

"Who are you?"

"Sorry sir," she mumbled, rubbing the sleep from her eyes.

"Sorry for what? I asked who you are." When she remained silent, he added, "Did you sleep here?"

Completely awake, she sprung up and ran out, a string of local dialects from the man behind her. She didn't understand what he was saying, but she clearly heard the word 'thief' somewhere in there, and the voice of a hysterical woman.

Another day of the same, and she began to think she would live out her life as a nomad, a broke nomad as she'd spent her balance on food and water.

Then she got her big break. A Hausa man speaking mangled English on the phone. She wouldn't have been interested in his vocabulary because living in the capital city for as long as she had, she was used to their funny way of pronunciation. What got her attention though, was the mention of 'Abuja' and it got better when he said, 'No, I will be there tomorrow morning, sir, we have already loaded the goods, oga."

And so, Kelechi spent the rest of the day stalking the man. In the evening, he and his partner climbed into the truck they had been hanging around all day and started the engine.

It was a struggle, but Kelechi managed to enter the truck right before it started its journey. Once in, it dawned on her that she hadn't made her plans well enough. Her fellow occupants were the last thing she expected.

SEVENTEEN

IT WOULD HAVE been fine to perch on the back door, it would have been OK to not even have entered at all, but the black eyes staring down at her was beyond her nightmares. To make matters worse, she had landed on her back, in cow dung. And worst, another came in. she saw it, from the way the tail wagged, the way it's hip muscles flexed, then out came its trophy, dung, aimed right at her face.

From what she knew, there were violent and nonviolent cows. The former would usually have a rope tied around its neck to warn people that they were fighters. Kelechi couldn't begin to count how many cows were in the trailer, but she saw three with ropes around their necks. Thankfully, they were at the inner end of the car, while she had landed at the rear end. Still, they eyed her. Two attempted to make their way to where she was, but with limited space, they gave up. But not the one with the red cord. It tried to come for her, and when it couldn't, it kicked the cow in its way, the cow ignored it but didn't move, so it kept kicking.

Kelechi huddled as close to the metal walls of the truck as possible, knowing that one kick from the cows, even the nonviolent, was all that was needed to end her life. *'How many hours to Abuja, or the nearest stop?'* she wondered. It was as if the universe already decided she was due to die, and all of these were just silly attempts from her side to hold on to a life she already lost.

Deciding that the cow was not going to bulge, the fighter cow turned on another to bully it out of the way. Unfortunately, it picked one which didn't have the patience of the previous cow. The bully kicked the new cow, the new cow returned the kick, and so a fight ensued. Kelechi was aware that she was the primary cause of the fight and wondered if the other cows would blame her. At this point, death by snakebite would've been a merciful death.

In the raucous, Kelechi failed to keep an eye on the other two, until it was too late. One was already a few paces away from her, and with the attention of the nearby cows on the fight, it was easy to moo them out of the way. Kelechi thought that she had seen it all, she thought that the events of the last few weeks had hardened her, but not when she was looking at sure death proceeding steadily towards her.

Then she screamed- a noise that cracked her voice and halted both the cows and the car.

Riding in the front seat squeezed between two men was a different shade of uncomfortable. If she said that it was bad, then she would be ungrateful. It was also half an hour ago when she screamed her lungs off until the car stopped and its driver raced out to know who was messing with, or possibly stealing their cows.

"Speak now before your head drop for ground." One of the men raised his machete over her head to drive his point home.

After the nightmare with the cutlass that she had witnessed, Kelechi was sure she had developed a phobia for blades.

"I just wanted to hitch a ride to Abuja." Kneeling before them, she pressed her hands together, begging for her life.

"How did you know our destination is Abuja?"

"I overheard your phone call in the evening."

"Why didn't you just come and asked us?" the one wearing a red knitted cap asked.

"I say we kill her here. This *yarinya* has another purpose here that she doesn't want to say," said the other.

"No please, there's nothing else- "

"Shut up there, who asked you to talk?" He tore his palm across Kelechi's face, a red flash blinding her for a moment.

"Don't hit her again! Don't you know she's a woman?"

The second man looked hurt that the other would deny him of such privilege. "She could be a thief!"

"How can she be a thief? One woman and how many cows?"

"She may be using jazz…"

"It's OK." To Kelechi he said, "Where are you going in Abuja?"

"I live in Maitama."

The man gave her a long look, then burst out in laughter, even the other one who'd slapped her narrowed his eyes at her. She then understood. Someone living in Maitama wouldn't dress as she was, or look unkempt, and most of all, a resident of Maitama would never need to catch a ride with cows. She didn't mind though that they doubted her, provided they left her alive, even right where she knelt on the highway, with bushes on both sides of the road and mountains carpeted by fog in the distance.

"Oya, come to the front, we will drop you at Kuje."

"Haba, the front seat cannot fit us both!"

"You will manage." Even Kelechi felt the command in his tune.

"Thank you so much," she said.

"She smells like shit," the other complained.

"Go bring water for her make she clean up."

The other man walked back to the car, dragging his legs as if they were infested by elephantiasis. It took a lot longer than it should have, but he returned with a sachet of water.

"One water cannot be enough, haba," the driver said.

"We no get water. Let her manage."

"Oya, madam, at least wash your face. We will be in Abuja by morning."

Kelechi used some leaves from the roadside weed to scrape the dung which had caked on her face, then washed her face and hands. She did not feel better, and neither did she smell better, but it was better than feeling the patch encrusted on her face.

"Thank you so much," she said.

Now here she was, breathing in the strongest and most repulsive body odor of her lifetime. It was already bad enough that she couldn't breathe in fresh air, but it was worse because she was practically crushed against the owner of the BO, the man who'd slapped her, and when the driver, the one with the red cap who'd invited her to ride with them, pushed the gear knob, which was very often, she was forced further back into the other man, who seemed to enjoy the body contact and made no move to adjust.

But then, it was much worse than having to share her personal space with a man cursed with BO, his mouth reeked too. More times than she could count, she had been in a constant threat of retching. And he seemed to constantly have something to say. But with each mile they covered, she was closer to home and true freedom.

"You want to eat?" to her surprise, it was the second man, who she would come to learn was named Ali, that offered.

Convinced that he couldn't have just changed his mind about hospitality, she said, "I don't have money."

"Don't worry, I will pay."

And so, she followed them out, into a roadside restaurant. It was around seven pm when they left Maiduguri, so she wasn't surprised when the clock in the restaurant read 3:47. It was 525 miles between Maiduguri and Abuja, and judging from the sixty to seventy miles they did and the incessant stops, she estimated she had just three more hours or so to be home. But that thought made her apprehensive. There just was no way nothing could go wrong and fling her to the farthest south.

The driver, Mustapha, conversed to his brother in Hausa, but she understood he told him that they'd rest a while before continuing. She didn't want to rest, she just wanted to get it over with, but it was not her call to make.

Ali bought them two plates of tuwo and soup. And from the disgusting way he ate, she decided she wasn't going to eat. Still, on their own accord, her hands went to work, first washing, then molding and dipping and directing to her mouth.

"Let us go back to the car," Ali said, after they'd eaten and rested a while.

It was only when they got to the car that Kelechi realized her mistake in following him.

He pinched her left breast. "Oya remove your cloth quick!"

"No ple…"

She didn't see his hand rise but heard his skin cracking her face and tasted the blood it drew even before she felt the sting of the slap. "Please," she repeated, tears welling in her eyes and spilling down her cheeks.

Ali grabbed her by her neck, squeezing hard. He brought her face up to his, "See it's no concern of mine if you're running from your husband or the people you are owing. I have given you a free ride to Abuja where you probably intend to start begging or whatever, and I have given you food. Now you will give me what I want, or I will kill you here and now."

"Please…" This time she saw the slap before it came, so she had time to brace herself.

"You think I am her to play or buff abi?" He hooked his palm on the neck of her shirt and ripped it into two. "Ha, you are one endowed bitch o!" He exclaimed in delight, looking at her breasts. The 36D she'd always been proud of now disgusted her. Worse, the force at which his first syllable came out and the closeness of his face to hers sent his bad breath straight to her senses. Her body disagreed with the odor, and she trashed to free herself from his grasp, but when he continued to press down by her shoulder, she lost control and puke rose and bathed him from the neck down.

His face contorted in rage and he shoved her down, one hand on her breast and the other undoing her jeans button while he pinned her down with the length of the arm whose palm cupped her left breast through her bra.

Then he fell limply on her.

"What is happening?" the driver asked.

Kelechi pushed Ali off her, and crawled away, still in tears, before speaking up, "He tried to… he was going to… he wanted … please save me!" She clasped the driver's hand.

"Ali, I have told you repeatedly that I will not interfere in whatever you choose to do, unless it's against a woman. Why will you even have the mind to hurt a woman when you have a mother, sisters, wives, and daughters? If another person do this to any of them, will you be happy?" But Ali cradled his head, the driver had hit him pretty hard. "I will go on to Abuja alone."

That got his attention, "What did you say? Haba, it has not gotten to that. I was only joking."

But minutes later, the truck was on the road again, with Kelechi alone in the front seat with the driver. Sensing that she felt guilty about his having to dump his brother, he engaged her in conversation to make her feel at ease. It worked, for in no time, Kelechi fell fast asleep.

"Yarinya, we have arrived," the driver tapped her awake.

Kelechi's heart drummed against her chest, and she couldn't control her shaking. She couldn't quite believe that she was in Abuja, she hadn't quite believed that she would see the capital city again in her lifetime. She climbed down from the truck, assisted by the driver who was already down and on her side of the door.

"I know you don't have any money, and I know you do not live in Maitama. I wish you luck." He gave her some cash. "Take this and take care of yourself as you find what to do here."

"Thank you so much," she said through tears.

"Ah don't cry, I cannot stand when women cry. I would have carried you to my house to stay until you sort yourself out, but I have a wife, and she will not like it."

"No, it's fine, I'll manage." She gave him a hug, not caring that his shirt was brown with dirt and smelled just as much. At least it was not like Ali's.

He had dropped her off at Kuje. She found it amusing that they didn't believe her, and she was glad that she found it funny. The old Kelechi who hadn't really seen life would have been offended.

Kelechi walked down the road, appreciating Abuja in a way that she never had. Darkness still blanketed the city, but the day had already started for many people. With the money she had, she could afford a cab, not that she couldn't have without the money. This was Abuja, she could easily get money from her house or office.

But it all started with a cab, so each time she lifted her arm to hail one, fear would grip her like a vice, and she would stop.

Something cold and sharp dug into her back. "If you move another inch, I will kill you," a gruff male voice said

EIGHTEEN

"OYA, GIVE ME everything you have."

Kelechi did, handing over the money the driver gave her. Now she was alone and as afraid for her life in the streets as in a cab.

A hint of golden had broken out in the sky, and soon, the corporate world would start. She needed to go away with her fears, at least until she got home. She was already in Abuja, and it made no sense to resume loitering, not when she had options.

The first cab she hailed stopped. She gave the driver her address as she settled in the passenger seat.

"Good morning o," he greeted, you could already tell that he was going to wear her ears off.

"Good morning," she replied. He rambled on, but she tuned him out, focusing her attention on the road they sped through. She tried to appear relaxed when she noticed her apprehension made the driver, an elderly man, uncomfortable. Still, she couldn't help it.

When the driver swerved into a different avenue, she clutched the steering, sending the car off the road and towards a group of girls going to school.

"What is your problem?!"

"Where are you going?"

"God, why did I meet a crazy woman this early in the morning?"

"I'm not crazy. I gave you my address and you're taking me somewhere else."

"Madam, I was going to buy petrol, you are my first passenger and I'm just coming out of the house, I haven't filled up."

"You should have told me."

"You are right, but you also should have asked me before you attempting to commit murder and suicide." He was right, so Kelechi kept her mouth shut. Finally seeing an opening for conversation, he pressed, "I noticed that you are not comfortable. Have you had any bad experiences with taxi drivers?" She didn't respond, but he wasn't fazed. "You know, as a commercial driver, I have heard many unbelievable stories."

Not interested in his stories, she turned her face out the window, and yelped in surprise. The face staring back at her from the side-view mirror wasn't hers. It was that of an older, leaner, and uglier woman. The hair was standing in all directions, the eyes had bags under them, and they were red, her lips were dry and parched, and her cheekbones jutted out like dislocated bones, and her face caked in dust. She was disgusting even to herself.

She turned away, afraid to look lower, and instead focused her attention on the road. In twenty minutes, she'd soak in a scalding hot tub and sleep for as long as she wanted.

They turned onto her avenue, but the closer they got, the jumpier she got. If only nothing else happened in 10,9,8,7…1. She was home.

"Wait here, let me get you your money."

"What are you talking about? You entered my cab without money to pay?"

"I'll just head into my house and bring your money for you. This is no big deal."

"You house? Shebi you want to play with me? That's why I don't carry certain people."

"Excuse me? What do you mean by certain people?" The driver didn't need to talk, he just looked her over. "Fine, I'm sorry, I should have told you. But just give me a minute."

"See, it's because this is early morning and I don't want trouble. Don't come out here and tell me that your madam refused to pay you."

"My ma…oh OK." She realized that he thought she was a help who worked for someone living in her estate. It made sense when you took her appearance in.

Her house key was in the bag she was carrying when she got kidnapped, but that didn't bother her. Even though there was no chance of someone as meticulous as her losing her keys, she kept a spare under her flowerpot.

It was already light enough at past six, but life hadn't begun in her estate, so she jogged the few meters up to her apartment which was the first house on the second block. All the while, the cab man observed her closely. She was tempted to change first and make herself a bit presentable to teach him not to judge people by their looks, but decided it wasn't worth the effort.

She found her keys exactly where and how she had expected, but she couldn't say the same for her house. The doorknob was broken, and she smelled cigarette smoke wafting from the crack.

A hand clamped over her mouth, even as she was whisked up into the air backward. This was the second time in less than an hour that she was being attacked from behind. The first, she hadn't fought back, but this time, it was her house, her city, and her choice. It was one thing when she was kidnapped without her knowing, it was one thing when she had been at a place where she neither knew the landmark nor understood the language, but here, on her own curb, she would not allow.

She bit the fingers clenched over her mouth so hard that she tasted blood. She didn't mind whose blood or think about the health implications. She had just one goal- to get him off her. But the hand didn't budge, only held tighter.

She raised her leg as high as it could go, and sent it down with force, aiming for her heels to contact the crotch of her abductor. But he anticipated the move and spread his legs before she could hit. She scratched and pinched, but he didn't stop for a moment, she may very well be an annoying insect.

"*Shhh,*" her assailant hissed, further riling her up. She had had enough of strangers messing with her life and treating her without civility.

She circled her arm around his neck and squeezed hard.

"Calm down woman. You fight like a cat!" It was Bem, her annoying neighbor, but before she could speak, he pinched her lips together. "There are men in your house." He stopped a moment, eyes unfocused, then grabbed her arm and shoved her into his car and entered after her.

"Easy, and what are you doing?" He didn't respond, instead, he took her lips in his own.

It was shocking in more ways than one, but he pressed her head to his face, making it impossible to free herself. The surprise threw Kelechi off balance. They had never been friends, much less, romantically involved. The driver who had been leaning on his door, started towards them, his face twisted in anger and disgust.

"I need to pay the driver," she said when he paused.

"Yeah? You got the money?" she looked down in shame. She had no money and telling him that she needed to pay the driver was like asking him to pay the driver. And seeing as they just kissed, it was also like he was paying for the kiss. But he was already removing a note from the wrap in his cockpit.

"How much is it?"

"Um, we really didn't negotiate."

He paused, "You entered a taxi without agreeing on a fare?"

His disapproving shake got her defensive. "It's not like I can't pay whatever amount." He raised his brows at her. "Well, he brought me to the house. All I needed to do was to enter and bring out his money."

The driver was already tapping on the window. He rolled it down and passed the note to him. "Thank you, oga." Then the driver looked at Kelechi and back at Bem, "Oga your taste in women sha…" Then he turned back.

"Thank you…"

"Do you know those men?"

He reached behind her as if to get something, so Kelechi could turn with him keeping up the pretense, but looking over his shoulder to her curb. There were military men standing around, while three more emerged. Two were smoking, and they were all looking at their direction. She broke out in a cold sweat. "No, I don't."

"You're sure?" But he didn't wait for her answer. The men were coming towards them, so he resumed the kiss. Later she'd wonder if she had kissed him back with such fierceness because she needed the soldiers to disappear, or because the first one had sent butterflies to her tummy and made her panty damp, and she was sad when he broke it. But at that moment, she didn't just kiss him back, she explored his mouth with her tongue, leaning in a lot too close, and hoping he'd take the lead and put out some of her fires with his hand.

He didn't, instead he broke the kiss again, leaving her with tightness in her chest, and emptiness and coldness where he had been.

"They are gone," he said.

Kelechi was disappointed and embarrassed. How could he not say something after what they'd just shared? She had never understood women who demanded that the man talks to them about 'it' whenever 'it' happened. She had thought them weak, and stupid. But now, she perfectly understood them it would have been OK if he had even said 'sorry', not that she wanted him to, but at least, it would mean that he was aware of whatever had happened. She would have asked him, except that she was scared that she was alone in her feelings. Again, she was in the shoes of the women she had classified as weak, who couldn't take the initiative to talk to the guy after 'it'. They were, in truth, the strong ones.

Her house was trashed beyond her recognition. She had begged him to go in first to make sure no men were left, but he refused, saying they were eleven that came in and the same number left. She wasn't convinced, but his argument was heavier, 'What if they come back to make sure, and you're in the car alone?' That was enough to get her to follow him instead.

Her table was turned upside down, her clothes were all on the floor where they'd obviously been stepped on. All open surfaces were carpeted with stuff from the closed surfaces. Her books were all taken down. Nothing was at its original place.

"You can't stay here." He took her hand and led her outside to his car. She barely saw through the tears blurring her vision, and her hands, like the rest of her body, were shaking. Bem strapped her in and drove off.

Everything in her life, including her life itself, was in chaos. She had fought death to be back, not expecting to see more of the same from over a thousand kilometers waiting for her even in her bathroom.

"Are you OK?"

It probably wasn't the question or her house, and maybe not the robbery or the attempted rape, or the episode with the cows. Then again maybe it was one of them or all of them combined. Kelechi couldn't control the scream that tore through her throat, so shrill and so alien that she thought it wasn't her voice.

Bem parked at a near-deserted area to let her cry it all out. He didn't offer her any tissue, assurance, kind words, or even the comfort of his shoulder. He just sat in the driver's seat and closed his eyes while she did what she needed to do.

Kelechi would stop crying, then almost immediately, a harder sob would follow, and the pattern repeated. Each scene from the last few weeks she recalled made her cry harder until her voice cracked, and her tears dry.

The sun in her face woke her up. She didn't know when he slept. Bem was still beside her, eyes focused ahead. "Thank you."

He was still for a moment, she didn't know him well, but she knew he was trying to get himself together. She recognized that much.

"Sleepyhead, finally decided to grace us with your consciousness?"

She wasn't interested in small talks. "Why did you do that?"

"Why did I kiss you?" It wasn't exactly what she meant. She meant everything— his stopping her from entering her apartment, his following her in to check things out, his giving her space to cry, and of course, the kiss. But the kiss was something she was very interested in. "Yes."

"Those men were coming out, I thought you wouldn't want them to see you, and I reasoned that they wouldn't want to disturb two lovers in heat."

Kelechi felt heat rise to her face and the area below her belt. But she wanted to hear the main reason. It was not like she was nice to him or anything.

"You must have noticed that my breath is bad. I haven't brushed in a long time." She didn't need to say that, but somehow she felt the urge to explain to him that she didn't always have bad breath. Like she was reassuring him that next time she'd taste better.

"Yeah, I noticed. Not only your breath, but the whole of you look and smell horrible." It was the perfect time for an earthquake, or maybe the kidnappers would launch a missile and blast them to hell. She wished she hadn't asked. But Bem had other things to talk about too. "Those men have been checking your house every few hours. Even asked some questions about you."

"What?"

"They said you're a threat to national security and whoever sees you should report to the police immediately."

"What? I am no security threat! What did they say I did?"

"Said it's classified, so we couldn't know."

"They are killers and murderers and human butchers, and assassins!"

"You know that basically, those words are synonyms of each other, right?"

"That's not the point." She turned to him. He was her neighbor, the handsome guy with a melting kiss. But that was all she knew about him. He may be taking her to… "Where are you taking me?"

"Nowhere. You gave me no destination so I'm just driving around."

"Really, you must believe me. I did nothing wrong; those guys are murderers."

"Relax, I'm not turning you in. I actually reported to the police the first time they broke into your house."

"You believe me?" She became even more suspicious. Why would he believe her just because she said so? "Why?"

"Well my dear, on a very basic level, no soldier would ask that we report to the police, especially seeing as you are a supposed national risk."

"But you said you reported them the first time, why would you report a soldier, especially without the army police mix?"

"They are not real soldiers," he said. He didn't even sound a bit unsure. "It is obvious if you know what you're looking for. For example, most of them had sound suppressors attached to their gun barrels. The military won't do that-only those on a mission to kill without rousing suspicions would. Also, a few of them didn't lace their boots with military artistic neatness. The military always have their boots laced, ready to be worn at any time, and real soldiers would lace their boots with the lace coming from the inside towards the outside, but some of these men had their boots laced in a mixture of crisscross and straight fashion and some of the eyelets were skipped which indicates it was buckled in a hurry by a possible amateur."

"How come you know all about the army?" His explanation about the guns and boots scared her. He wouldn't know all of those if he didn't belong. Kelechi couldn't successfully smooth over the suspicion in her voice.

"OK, first, I noticed two of them were wearing their gun holsters on the left instead of on the right side of the hip with the grip pointing backward, that's just never done, and it roused my suspicion. They claim to have come from the barrack but they had mud caked on their boots. That's an indication that they had come from a place farther than the barracks, probably crossed some muddy water or drying pond."

Bem took in her stoic face, the grim line digging into her forehead and fanning out at the sides of her mouth. "Do you have somewhere you'd like me to take you?"

"Yes please." She gave him her office address. The only other place she had was her cousin's. Her Mom and siblings lived out of town, and even if they lived in, she still wouldn't go there. She did not want to endanger them in any way. She had nowhere else.

She had him stop in the office block after hers, then walked back to hers through the second gate where her staff never took as it was a longer trek. It wouldn't do for anyone who knew her to see her the way she was. She navigated through the building, following offices she knew opened late, until she made a turn that took them directly to the back door of her office, where the first door she would meet was Lucy's. No one was there and Kelechi wondered whether she should be glad or furious that Lucy had become lax in her absence.

Her office door was unlocked, and when she entered, the sight greeting her left her speechless.

"You are not supposed to be here," Lucy said, reaching for the phone.

Bem was by Lucy's side in three long strides. He grabbed her wrist, "You will not make that call."

When they entered, she was sitting on Kelechi's chair, leg propped up on her table, and eating out of a box of pizza. But most embarrassing, she wore just boxers and a brown singlet that clearly outlined her south faced breasts. "You don't understand, this woman is a criminal!" With her free hand, she snatched a towel from the armrest and attempted to cover her chest. Kelechi was strict about office conduct, and what her office was reduced to was almost as bad as being robbed.

"Who were you trying to call?"

"This is a matter of national security," she said to Bem, deliberately ignoring Kelechi.

"They got here too?" Kelechi felt a tightening in her chest. They had been monitoring her home, turned her workers into a spy for them, there was little doubt that they'd gone to her family too. She prayed they were safe.

"Really, you didn't think that if they traced you to your house then going to your place of work was basically reasonable?"

"You brought me here!" she said to him, annoyed that he'd take that tone with her.

"I didn't know this was your office, I'd have advised you against it. I believed you knew better."

He was right, she didn't know better. She turned to her secretary, "What are you doing in my office?"

"Ha, you left for how many weeks. Someone had to take charge."

She wanted to ask if taking charge meant replacing all her personal effects and turning her office into a food smelling junk house, but she played it cool. "I am back, now get out of my chair."

"I am sorry, *lady*, you don't call the shots here anymore. I am in charge now, and you are a wanted woman. I wonder what crime you committed. They said it's classified, but I won't disbelieve if they come up with some psychopathic things like killing and stashing bodies."

Kelechi was dumbfounded, it was Bem that spoke. "I know she's mean, but come on, she can't be that bad." He was smiling.

She chose to overlook them. "Guys, this is serious, I mean these guys are murderers."

"So, you said, but here you are, all in one piece."

"I have evidence. They kill men, women, boys, girls, and children. *Pregnant women.* I've seen it with my own eyes!"

"You said you have evidence?" Bem's voice was hard.

Lucy glanced at her necklace; she knew that it was a recording device. "I don't care, I am not giving up this position, I have an official claim to it."

She may have an official claim, but so did Kelechi, but, she was not interested in the position. "Lucy, I am telling you that people are dying every hour, don't you care about that?"

That got Lucy, but she didn't want to back down easily. "Or you may be a criminal trying to do more awful things."

"You said you have evidence," Bem said again.

"I do if she'd let me use the computer."

Lucy would have argued further, but one step towards her that Bem took had her moving out of the way to let Kelechi pass. But as Kelechi said, 'thank you', she pinched her nose closed. It was embarrassing, especially the obvious extra effort that Lucy took to avoid body contact with Kelechi.

"You look like you crawled out of a pigsty," she mumbled, low enough that you knew it was a mumble, yet loud enough to be heard by all.

Kelechi ignored her and took a seat. It felt good to be back in something familiar. She detached the pendant to insert the USB to her computer. The wallpaper was different, replaced by a hideous pink background.

As if on cue, the phone rang. She made to pick out of reflex, but Lucy put her hand over hers. Kelechi let it go.

"Hello, Phoenix Reviews, how many I help you?"

Her eyes widened, and she turned to face Kelechi. Bem got to work. He took a pen from the table and scribbled on the back of a file, then held it up to Lucy. '*Play it cool. Don't tell them she's here*', it read.

"OK," she said to whoever was on the other line. "I will call you as soon as I hear or see anything." A pause, then she said, "Oh, no one here would do that. They all hate her even more than I do." She drummed a hand on the table, let out a deep breath, then said again, "Sir, I understand, I will talk to my team." And she hung up.

"That was a great performance," Bem said, "You didn't even look like you were acting."

"I have had enough practice," she said, scowling at Kelechi.

"What did he say?" Kelechi asked.

"He was reminding me to call him when there's news about you. Reminding me to tell my team to act cool and normal if they see you and asking if I need his help to educate them! He also said that he had reasons to believe that you're headed to town if you aren't here already." The force which she added to every 'remind' and 'educate' had Kelechi wincing. It probably was because of her, and she felt uneasy at the thought.

"Thanks for not telling," Kelechi said.

"It's not for you, I wouldn't care less what they do with you. I did this in case your story is true. I'd call him back in a heartbeat if your evidence is lacking."

"It is, I swear."

"Then bring it on already. You're wasting time." Bem said.

"And talking about time, it's a workday, and the team members will start arriving at any moment. We need to get ready for business, and I need to freshen up and arrange this place. You could do with that advice too." Lucy took her time to look Kelechi from head to toe, to emphasize her point.

They stood behind her as she fast-forwarded to the point where she tried to negotiate with the taxi driver, then to the fight she had with him. When Mr. Kimaiyo came up, Lucy exclaimed that he was the soldier who had spoken to her, and when he shot the driver, both she and Bem knew that it was going to be a tough clip.

He reached over her shoulder and paused it. "What time will your staff start coming?"

"Any moment from now." Both women answered.

"OK, we don't know if they would decide to send men over here to check for themselves. We need this place as normal as possible. Kelechi, you can use the restroom here, right?"

She wanted to say 'of course, it was her restroom', but she looked at Lucy for approval.

"Of course, " she stuttered, then she decided she gave in to easy. "But I have to use it first because when she's done, I'd need to have the place sanitized."

"Fair enough," Bem said. You girls go freshen up, then Lucy, call a staff meeting when everyone is here. It would be better if everyone sees this together and is on the same page, then we can decide our next move."

Kelechi liked how everything was going as if with a purpose, but she didn't dare hope.

"Where are you going?" she said as Bem turned towards the door.

"To get you something to change in. My dear, you stink." And he left.

It may have been in the tone he used which did not suggest that he meant that as an insult, but Kelechi found herself smiling at the remark. Lucy frowned at her, then shook her head and left.

With nothing to do, Kelechi took the opportunity to review what was on the table. Nothing was as she insisted, they be kept, and the reviews and plans were not as they'd have been written by her, but they weren't bad either.

***

Once outside, Bem brought out an old phone, punched in some numbers and held it to his ear. At the grunt of a voice on the other end of the line, he said, "The eagle has perched, await my instructions." Then he continued down the block until he found a boutique.

NINETEEN

EVERYTHING MOVED TOO fast for Kelechi to keep track of. When she emerged from the bathroom, a very flattering blue dress was resting on the back of her chair. It fit her figure, being provocative without revealing anything. on her own, she would never have picked such outfit, but she liked how beautiful it made her feel. Coupled with the black strap four inches sandals he bought with it; she felt the closest she could to confident.

"Conference room three." Lucy was by the door, observing her with a veiled expression.

"Is everyone there?"

"Yes."

Lucy turned to go but Kelechi ran and stood in front of her outside the door, successfully halting her. " Wait!"

"What else can I do for you?"

Kelechi wasn't used to the older woman talking to her that way and she wasn't sure how to respond to it. "Um, nothing?"

"I figured, now let's go, I'll like to have my life back on track."

"I'm sorry- "

"What's that?"

"Really, I am. My career was so important to me that I lost sight of things that matter. I was horrible to you guys. I knew that even then, but you must understand that I was grooming you all while moving the company forward. I couldn't afford to be soft."

"You just didn't want to be nice- soft is a stretch- you could be nice and still achieve your ambitions."

"Right now, I want to give 'nice' a shot, if you'd help me."

Lucy narrowed her eyes. "You are being this way because you want me to give up your position easily?"

"Come on, Lucy, we both know it wasn't up for argument. It is mine and will always be."

"First, you have to get yourself out of whatever it is you're in."

"Thank you!" Kelechi reached out for a hug, but Lucy drew back.

"No o! You'll need at least ten dozen thorough bathing before I can afford that."

"If you're both quite done can we start now?" Bem said. He was standing by the door of the conference room. Kelechi felt her body begin to shake. Bem's mien was alien; so hard and frightening. Lucy noticed.

"Not quite," she said to him then turned to Kelechi. "I think I have a couple sanitary pads remaining. Come let's check." Bem opened his mouth to talk, but Lucy already dragging Kelechi back into the office.

"Sanitary pad?" whispered Kelechi when they were alone in the office and the door firmly shut behind them.

"Yeah, you looked like you were about to faint. What's the deal with him?"

Kelechi was surprised at the confident take-charge Lucy facing her. "He's my neighbor."

"Is he to be trusted?"

"I don't know. He saved me when I returned, and the killers were in my apartment. But I can't afford to trust anyone right now. Those men are heartless!"

"Well, we can't get rid of him now, we can't call the police or even the army. I think the best thing to do right now is to make this public immediately, that way both the good and bad guys sees it. You said the video has enough evidence?"

"It has more than enough. What you saw is not even the main deal. Those men kill more than five people per day!"

Kelechi watched myriad of emotions chase themselves across Lucy's face. The older woman staggered and would have landed on her butt if not for Kelechi's supportive arm around her.

"You don't know these people's reach Lucy-"

"Let's pray about it and leave it to God." Without waiting for her consent, Lucy took Kelechi's hands and bowed her head, already calling on the Almighty. In a way, she reminded Kelechi of Ifeoma.

Remembering her filled Kelechi with a wave of sorrow, she shut her eyes trying to quell the emotions threatening to submerge her, but that only brought on more memories of each of the hostages she met, even those she never exchanged words with. By now, all of them would have been killed, replaced by new victims, and the cycle continues. Kelechi slipped her hands off Lucy's and knelt and broke into tears which were further replaced with unknown tongues. After all of this was over gone, she would not believe she had prayed in the Holy Spirit. Lucy knelt with her and engulfed Kelechi in a much-needed hug while also praying with her.

When they were done, they found Bem at the door of the office, his expression still hard and unreadable. He said, "Let's get this over with."

After the session with God, Kelechi felt perfect peace deep within her soul, it was as though a gray drape had been covering the sun since her kidnap and was only just lifted. Everything seemed brighter and smelled better, even her armpit.

"OK," she said to Bem, this time without reservation. She hadn't made it this far because she was careful. God had been involved after all. She looked at Lucy and the woman nodded, a silent pledge of allegiance. Later, in her quiet moments, Kelechi would wonder at the evil in the world and the equal goodness therein too. She'd marvel at how she had closed her eyes and heart to this virtue that she'd come to realize was an actual strength.

Bem led the way and she followed, tailed by Lucy, Kelechi was quick to notice her confidence restoring, even though she wore plastic slippers as her feet were too blistered for the shoes.

As soon as they entered the conference room, everyone took up their phones, punching away like their lives depended on it.

And that was when Bem whipped out his gun.

TWENTY

FEAR IS NOT a feeling; it is tangible and real — like the ghosts who watches over you at night. It is as alive as the demons caged inside you. Everyone has that being living in them, eating and sucking away at their soul and essence, until all you are is a husk housing fear.

Lucy was instantly on the floor, hand over her head, legs flailing up behind her. All thirty-seven full time staff in Phoenix Review stopped the phone action; some dropping, others clenching, while some just held the poor devices. Eyes were already watering, mumbles of prayers forming a hum, and everyone trembling.

Perhaps when you have watched humans slaughtered, birthed babies who you were sorry for even while they were still in an unsafe womb, been 'hugged' by a snake, hunted, peed on, nearly raped, kissed death more than a million times. When you have been chased into another country, smelt decaying bodies, stolen worn slippers, impersonated, farted on by cows and being run down, you understand how to not just face the fear in you, but own it and wear it. Become as fearless as the fear.

Kelechi didn't even miss a heartbeat; she didn't feel afraid because she had donned fear. She walked around to him. "So, you were them after all." It wasn't a question; it was a statement made from a place of calm.

The young man lowered the gun, ran a finger lovingly across its golden case, took it up to his nose for a long whiff, then gave it a kiss. "Because of this?" He waved the gun at Kelechi. "Now, I won't give anyone a headache if you don't give me cause to." He walked around the table collecting all the phones, then returned. "Really Lucy, you don't want to dirty that lovely shirt. Come take a seat."

Kelechi acted fast or thought she did-carrying the camera stand at her corner to smash him with, but Bem turned before she completely hefted it. "You really don't want to do that."

"Yeah? I may die within seconds, but you go before me." She swung down but Bem stepped out of range.

"Really, woman, I'm not part of them."

"Yeah right, I am not part of the kidnapped either."

"I promise you; the gun was so that no one would call them here. You think if I'd told them not to, any of them would have listened? It was more effective with the gun."

"I don't believe you."

"You don't have to; you just have to trust the guy who kissed your smelly mouth to save you from the very group you accuse him of being a part of."

That did the job. Kelechi lowered her head in shame. Even Lucy had the audacity to chuckle.

"Hey, I still enjoyed the kiss regardless, though I'd prefer we do it next time only after you've given your hygiene real attention."

The topic wasn't going well in her favor, she had to shift it. "Explain why you have a gun then."

"Ah this." He resumed caressing the metal, "this was a gift from a man I respect so much that I'd die for him in a heartbeat."

"Mr. Kimaiyo?"

"Oh please, I already told you I'm not part of that group." His tone was still on the same octave, but his voice was tight, although not as tight as his face. Kelechi wasn't fazed though.

"But- "

"I am part of a group dedicated to hunt your men down. I'm a special OP, specially trained group not working directly with the government, not working for an individual but for another group who you could call the Godfathers of Africa. The Nigerian division."

"I don't understand a thing."

"You are not meant to; however, this is the most I can say, and I'm only saying this, so you understand that I'm not your enemy."

"But you have to ex- "

"I'd have to kill you all if I said more than I have. Now let's get to it, ladies and gentlemen, please calm down, Kelechi has something to tell all of us." He took the head seat, commanding it like he owned it. Kelechi wanted to smack his head.

Kelechi took her time to look at every member of her team, in their eyes she found varying emotions from fear to hate to awe. Later she'd come to know that most of those reactions were based on their certainty that her return meant that their paycheck would go back to standard, and workload would also increase exponentially. Yet knowing that didn't make her not resize the salaries that Lucy had taken advantage of her absence to increase, nor would it make her task them less, instead she added more—reaching families who's lost loved ones and making their voices heard a big part of

Phoenix Review. However, she would begin to listen to them more, to see them, not just look at them, to become involved whenever she could, and to smile often.

"On the morning that I was supposed to go to Aso Rock, I was kidnapped by a taxi driver who was working for a horrible group," she started. She saw Isaac roll his owl eyes and turned his face away. Isaac had rebelled against her the most, especially after she cut paychecks and still insisted on sending him to cover news even during the weekends. He had argued that he had a family that needed his presence at least at weekends and that the salary decrement affected them hugely. Kelechi had told him to quit if he wasn't going to accept the terms and he had chosen to stay but became bitter towards her. Today was however not the day to put him in his place. So much was at stake.

"That is what you say, but the authorities are saying a totally different thing," Tega, her newest camera crew member said. Kelechi liked him; he was ambitious and said little.

Kelechi unwound her necklace and removed the pendant. "Most of you know what this is. It took in everything, at least everything that my eyes saw." She nodded at Lucy who dimmed the lights. Kelechi inserted the USB into the laptop and connected to the projector. The scene began with her reflection in the mirror in her bedroom, then the episode with Bem. Her wait for a taxi, the drive, the struggle. And when the driver was shot, Zoe sprang up from her chair as if it was ablaze. The video speed was increased as there were long moments where no event took place and even when it did, no one wanted to know the details. When they got to camp, Kelechi noticed Isaac sitting up—his subconscious reaction when you had his full attention.

In the darkness they couldn't see what lay with Kelechi, but she wasn't bothered, morning would come eventually, and it did, giving them an uncomfortable close with the bodies even the ones Kelechi hadn't dared to look at. When Kelechi turned to the chop block most of them were already on their feet. This time Kelechi watched with them and through the tears that blurred her vision, she saw the same running down faces of men and women of her team. Nneoma, the cook had her eyes covered but she watched through the cracks between her fingers, very quick to press them together when she sensed action. Overall, most stood and turned away after the death of the help. If only they knew that the worse lay ahead. Lucy came up and wrapped her hands around Kelechi as the young woman sobbed. Kelechi still couldn't believe any of what happened even though she had been there. She wondered why she was alive, what she did to merit it. She was delusional; she knew she was not the best-behaved person on earth. Nneoma came up to her from behind, hugging her—even though all Kelechi really felt was her excess bosom pressed against her head. Soon, she was lost amid the bodies that rushed to hug her, indeed just a few people stood back, and she wasn't sure if they were all embracing her to offer comfort or take in strength from the enfold— taking and receiving, all in tears.

"Um guys!" It was Tega, apparently, he had been calling for a while, but his voice was drowned by sobs. "We have a problem."

"What is it?" Isaac asked, veins popping from different parts of his face.

"I called the military man that asked us to contact them when we saw Kelechi."

"You what?"

"Hey, there was no way I could have known!"

"It's too late, they're already here," Bem said.

TWENTY-ONE

ALL HELL BROKE loose. From screams to prayers followed by tears, everyone running helter-skelter.

"We have to leave," Zoe said, she was already having a panic attack, shaking vigorously.

"You can't, they'll assume you know something, and you will be terminated instantly," Bem said.

"Can't they pretend it was a false alarm?" Kelechi asked.

"Sorry Hun, your crew may be good at lying, but trust me, they are not that good. One person may manage to be convincing, but not when everyone here knows the truth. They'd smell you from a mile away."

"We can all run away through the backdoor," someone suggested.

"Yes, you can, but you won't escape. I guarantee that we are surrounded, plus don't freak out, but they already have all your data, including your family and friends' lists."

"Is there good news somewhere in there?" Kelechi asked.

Zoe continued rambling, while sitting on the bare floor. "My wedding is in two weeks. I don't want to die. I'm an only child. Why did you people drag me into this?"

Bem turned away made a call no one understood. "My squad is almost here."

"Does it mean we'll live?" Isaac asked.

"I can't guarantee that. Our primary mission is to get the killers."

"So, you'll leave us all to die?" Lucy asked.

"There's no guarantee for our own lives. Those men are expertly trained, and they are ruthless. I am confident that we can match them there, but their advantage is that they have no care for civilian lives, they could start a shootout, and we would need to avoid that."

"You have the advantage of surprise," Tega said.

"Yes, we do, but they will also prepare for that. It's basic."

"So, they win? After I've made it this far?" Kelechi was angry. "Do you have any idea how close I've been to death in the last six weeks? Do you know what I've gone through? I stole worn out slippers and N400! I impersonated a Reverend Sister, I slept with an old man who looked worse than the ugliest. I have been pooped on by cows and rode with the worse BO. I've been bitten by a snake then almost died thanks to a medical nurse accomplice. You really cannot imagine it even if you watch it on tape. Now, I am home just to be killed by the same men?"

"It won't be in vain. I'll transfer the recording to our headquarters so that whatever happens they will be taken down. You have saved countless people today, Kelechi."

Tega ran forward pushing both aside. "What are you doing?" Lucy asked.

"If we will die, we'll go in a grand style. I'm sorry Bem, but I don't really trust you."

"What do you have in mind?" Kelechi asked, as he punched commands into the computer.

"I'm uploading this video to the main server and cloud; it will be sent to every outlet we command in three hours unless we stop it."

"Make it automatically go viral?" Kelechi already liked the idea.

"Exactly. We just need to find a scene that'll grab people's attention."

"You don't know what you're doing!" Bem was horrified.

"Mr., you don't call the shots here. Tega use as much funds as you need," Kelechi said.

"Yes ma'am."

"We should also send it to other news channels; this is much more than PR now, also foreign intelligence."

"Do it," Kelechi said, and Lucy took the next computer. "Set it to deliver as Priority One in six hours." Through it all, Kelechi still thought like a businesswoman. If Phoenix Review's didn't get suppressed, it'd give her the exclusive she deserved. "Send to the bloggers in five hours. They can set the stage for the big channels." It was more than that, bloggers were the hardest to suppress and the most dangerous—the little ants you couldn't fell in one big swoop, you need to track them down one after the other and before you get to them all, they would have already caused you crippling damage.

Isaac was also at another computer. "Setting 360 angles to every CCTV in the office. One button push and we'll be live to any open receiver," he reported. It was the real reason why Kelechi didn't fire him through his act-ups; he was the best at what he did.

Soon everyone who had something to contribute was on it. The preemptive was mind boggling. Here were men and women possibly facing the last moments of their lives, yet they choose to use it for the greater good—no one spoke of wills or calling families—even Zoe was typing away at forming the perfect article to go with the video. Her works usually needed editing for tenses, but she was an amazing writer. Tega selected the scene where the head was chopped and a still image of the bodies. Kelechi added the image of the baby taken and the mother being led away. Even if they died, soon, even the streets would not be safe for the killers. Everyone will have a common enemy and there would be nowhere to hide.

"My squad is surrounding us," Bem announced. It wasn't necessary as his words were echoed by shot after shot. "You can't remain here, where is the best extraction point?" There was no other than the way they'd come. Bem issued more coded commands into his old phone and soon the shots were heavier out back than front. "We are trying to lure them away from there, it's tricky and may fail, but we're hoping that they'd be less worried about catching you since it is obvious we're onto them."

"But won't they get mad and go after my family?" Zoe's face was a mess. She'd always been a heavy face painter and with the tears her eyeliner ran mixing with her foundation, revealing zits riddled face.

"Soldiers have been dispatched to each of your close families, but that's as thin as we can afford to stretch."

"How about Frankie? He's close family too, he's paid my dowry."

"Yeah, Frankie too." Kelechi heard the lies in his words but thankfully the reassurance seemed to be enough for Zoe.

"But the soldiers can't be trusted. Those killers were soldiers too. They even encouraged us to call soldiers."

"Because they were going to intercept the call whoever you called." The shots were moving. "Let's go!"

TWENTY-TWO

"GOOD MORNING, MUMMY." Kelechi had no intentions of getting out of bed any time before noon, but then her mother had to assault her senses with the aroma of jollof rice—who cooked rice for breakfast? Oh, she knew; her mum.

"God bless you. You aren't dressed? You'll be late for work." Kelechi felt dizzy at the thought of going to work, instinctively she went to the windows to peep. "Not even one reporter," her mother said. They had been flocking her like a bee. Now she had a firsthand experience what it was like for those public figures they hounded.

"It has been a hard few months."

"Which is why you should get out there. No one should go through what you went through, but please don't let me lose you to it. You can't coop in my house forever."

"I'm scared, Mummy." It felt good speaking it out.

"It's OK to be scared. I'm scared too, especially as not all those killers have been put away. I'm also scared at the thought that there may be others like them. But what I'm most scared of is that you may never move past this. Please, my darling, you promised me baby steps, remember?"

"Mamma…"

"You promised today. We have been preparing for this day. Be the achiever I've always known."

"I'll go to work today, Mummy." Kelechi couldn't hold it in much longer, she lunged at the food. She really was becoming a food grubber.

After a few spoons she lost her appetite. Everything was still a blur, from their extraction to Bem taking them to an unknown fortress. Kelechi had fought him all the way until he knocked her out. When she came to, she began screaming, the sound high pitched and shrill. She wasn't going to quietly sit in any buildings with tower fences. Then someone covered her nose with a citrus smelling cloth, and she passed out again. When she woke this time, she was in a hospital where she was told she'd been out for 3 days. Soldiers armed to their teeth stood around the room and she would have resumed screaming except that all her family members were there including her mother and the Reverend Father from the village. He had heard the news and came — along with thousands of people to see her. He wouldn't have been allowed in except that the video showed him, and he was a Reverend. All through her hospital stay, Kelechi never had a moment of privacy; one government official or dignitary came after the other. Her staff, boss, even passing acquaintances. Then there were the ever-present soldiers and her mother who seemed to have a permanent place at her bedside. Even when she went to the bathroom, her mother would come in if she stayed for more than a couple of minutes. It was the stifling that made her insist to go home.

But she couldn't enter her house even though it'd been cleaned and arranged. Thus, she went to her mother's house. The reporters, new fans, and even families of hostages who wanted to hear about their loved ones from her personally—never mind that she probably didn't meet the said loved ones or may be had but did not exchange words with them. Then hostages who had been released coming to thank her, none of whom were the ones she'd been in the camp with.

Kelechi stood a minute longer before her mirror. All the pants she tried on fell off her waist, even the few skirts she owned. Now she stood in a gown that was once her size, but now hung on her unflatteringly at six sizes larger. She didn't feel inclined to touch her face, but she had done it anyway, after all 'normal' was the language she needed to speak.

Her mother was all smiles as she emerged from her room, yet through the smile, Kelechi saw the dread and so upped her own smiles. Her mother's health wasn't what it used to be, and she worried at what toll all this took on her.

"Good morning." Bem was at the door holding a bunch of flowers out to her. "Your mother told me you were ready."

She wasn't, but she wasn't going to let it show. "Yeah. I have a company to run."

"I'm your ride and I'm ready when you are."

"Um, no thanks." He looked handsome in gray suits, but it was his smile and the way her eyes seemed engrossed to his lips that bothered her, however not as much as entering the car.

"That didn't come out right, I guess. It's not an option, I'm your personal security for now."

"For what?"

"For security."

"Look Bem, I did-"

"You can drive, but that's as far as negotiation goes." He leaned closer blessing her with a nose full of heady scent. He smelled like the dust that wafted from the sand at the first drop of rainfall after a long dry season. He made an effort. "Oh, and the car's yours, courtesy of the Godfathers."

Kelechi stepped out of the house to see her new car.

"Did you read my diary?" The car was exactly the ride she dreamed of owning, down to the color.

"Kind of." As her face turned up, he brought up his palms. "It's not like that. It was after the killer's first visit. I was looking for a way to track your whereabouts down."

"Oh." She inhaled the scent of the flowers. "Thank them for me." It was amazing how things which would originally excite her seemed fickle to her, but then, things she'd been immune to seemed to control her — like Bem's lips and the memories it brought, both wanted and unwanted. "Did you get what I asked?"

"Yes." He handed her a note with addresses and phone numbers. She would track down Ifeoma's and Ekanem's families whatever it took. Among those that'd come to her, she had expected them. It was understandable why

Ekanem's family wouldn't, maybe Ifeoma's husband didn't come because he resented her for birthing his child to be killed, but she wouldn't know unless she went.

"So, you want to date?"

It was probably the simplicity at which he asked or maybe she wanted to experience that kiss again, but Kelechi found herself nodding. "Yes."

AUTHOR'S NOTE

A Touch of Reality is more than a work of fiction for me. A Touch of Reality is a cry, which I hope will reach the right ears.

To every victim of kidnap; both for ransom, and Kelechi's type of kidnap: I pray for a way out for you.

To everyone who lost their lives to kidnappers: I am sorry we failed you.

To everyone who has lost someone; acquaintance, colleague, friend, family: I remember you.

To those who are at the verge of turning bad; hang in there. Do not take that step. In its path lies destruction, pain, and unhappiness.

To kidnappers and killers who are there not by choice; you can always do something. Remember Ekanem. He may be fictitious, but you can borrow his courage.

To kidnappers and killers who began by choice but now want out; you can make this right. You can always redeem yourself. There is no sin too great for God to forgive.

To kidnappers and killers who derive joy in other people's pain; do not forget that a day of reckoning will always come.

To agents and mercenaries of criminals: that person you are victimizing is someone's special one. It could be yours tomorrow.

To the law enforcers; we recognize your efforts, we only ask that you do more.

To the government; we understand that fighting crime is no easy feat, but we are trusting you to safeguard our lives and properties. Please try harder. Every single life matters.

To Leah Sharibu; we will never forget.

To the general public; every life is a life. 'be your brother's keeper' is a collective responsibility.

ABOUT THE AUTHOR

Best Nwachinemere is a Nigerian based writer whose works have appeared in a number of anthologies.

She got her first degree in political science at National Open University of Nigeria.

Best is a schoolteacher who divides her time between drafting lesson notes and writing stories. When not doing either of those, she would be found at the nearest bookshop.

www.ingramcontent.com/pod-product-compliance
Lightning Source LLC
Chambersburg PA
CBHW020911160726
47993CB00005B/1921